SOUL DEEP

Monique Gilmore

Pinnacle Books
Kensington Publishing Corp.

http://www.pinnaclebooks.com

PINNACLE BOOKS are published by

Kensington Publishing Corp.
850 Third Avenue
New York, NY 10022

Pinnacle, the P logo, and Arabesque are Reg. U.S. Pat. & TM Off.

First Printing: May, 1997
10 9 8 7 6 5 4 3 2 1

Printed in the United States of America

This book is dedicated to

FAMILY & FRIENDS
both *old* and new,
who have been INSTRUMENTAL along my journey
and have helped me when things
were not fun but TOUGH.
I appreciate all that you've
done.
Thank You.

NJ: Sheila D. Lewis, Randy Alston, Alan & Zelina Mitchelle, Tonya Sindab, Alan Anderson, Denise McDaniels.

NY: Richard O'Neal.

CO: Aunt Caroline & Uncle Tony Phillips, Melonie Wilson, Paul T. Deaderick, Tessa Alexander, Clare Villarosa, M&D's Restaurant, Rena Shead, Deborah Shead, Darryl Clarke, Happy Hanes, Khadeshi Hanes, Mrs. Hanes, Ezra Johnson, Rhonda Craighton, Delta Sigma Theta—Denver Alumni Chapter.

MI: Kym Wells, D.R. Angie Borders-Robinson, Aaron Robinson, Nanette Williams, Rochelle & Jim Hurst.

CA: Brian & LeAnne White, Sandi Reid & Leon Johnson, Michelle Harris, Brenda & Walter Wilson, Robin Deane, Uncle Bee-Bop, Sonya Crockett, Debra Shaw, Fremont Bible Fellowship, Alan Mitchell, Ed Jones, Deborah Boykin.

GA: Donzel & Charlene Rosenberg, Traci Rucker, Maury Harris.

DC: Janis Hazel.

Special Thanks to:

Doug Sayers—NAS Miramar Public Affairs Officer, San Diego, CA. Thank you for adding the authentic "touch." Your expertise with the military jargon and procedures was invaluable.

John McCorkel—deejay, KKSF 103.7 FM, San Francisco, CA. Thank you for taking time, while on the air on July 6, 1996, to help me find "that song," by George Winston.

Cheryl Ferguson—literary reader/reviewer, SC. I reallllllly appreciate your encouraging words and prayers. Thank you so much for our "brainstorming" sessions. Anxiously awaiting my first historical read.

Crissena Coleman—journalist, New York, NY. As if you don't have enough stuff to read and write. Thank you for your support. Looking forward to purchasing your book.

One

Marietta, Georgia

Yvonne Taylor hustled onto her future in-laws' front porch, shaking her head free of the few snowflakes that had drifted into her hair during the short walk from the driveway. The peephole to the double oak doors was covered with a lavender, soggy piece of paper with the words *Come on in* streaked in blue marker pen.

She inhaled a chilled breath, letting it flow out slowly, as she read the sign a second time. Even in the frigid temperature, and with a pair of cashmere-lined leather gloves, she felt perspiration on the palms of her hands. *Ridiculous.* How was she going to live the rest of her life in fear of what awaited her on the other side of the door? It was an engagement party for her and her fiancé, Desmond, for Christ sake. How much could go wrong in the space of three hours? Pulling off her gloves, she wiped her hands against her wool coat, then pressed down the lever. Hesitantly she pushed open the door and stepped inside.

"Well, I heard that Liz can't stand Yvonne's behind," one lady was saying to another in a whispered voice. "She told me if she had anything to say about it, she would prefer that Desmond marry his old girlfriend, Danni, than marry Yvonne."

"Yeah, I heard the same thing," the other lady said. "I guess Liz just feels that no matter how hard Yvonne tries, she'll never be of the same stock as her son. I hear that Yvonne's father was some so-called kind of jazz musician-slash-drug fiend before he died. Her father's sister practically raised her."

"Where's her mother?"

"Died in childbirth, I heard."

"What a shame," the heavyset one said, shaking her head. "Liz doesn't think Yvonne's as smart as she tries to be. I heard she failed the bar twice."

"Nooo," the other lady sang.

"Yesss," Yvonne mimicked aloud, startling the two women. These hussies have their nerve, she thought, eyeing them both. "Anything else you'd like to know about me or my family or my personal business?"

The two women stood still and at a loss for words. Incensed, Yvonne cut her glare away from them. She brushed past them toward the living room, where a swaying banner hung above. Visions of pink Bermuda sand crawling between her and Desmond Rappaport's toes were evaporating briskly. Living anywhere other than a four-hour plane ride away from Liz Rappaport, Desmond's mother, and her two-bit bourgeois friends, would not suffice.

Yvonne stood in the foyer, observing the oversized banner. *Congratulations Desmond and Yvonne!* How special. She let out a troubled breath before scanning the room, which was packed with guests, for Desmond. A glass of white zinfandel would help her to relax—loosen her up before she came face to face with Liz, her aggravating future mother-in-law. An unexpected hand rested atop her shoulder. She jumped.

"Where you been, girl? 'Bout time you got here," the

tall, thin, light-complected man said to her. "Let me get your coat for you."

"Hey, Mr. Rappaport," Yvonne said playfully. She patted the remaining speckles of snowflakes from her forehead with the end of her silk scarf. "You know how these Georgia drivers are when there's a lick of snow on the ground. They're disastrous."

"Yeah, I know." He smiled, helping her out of her coat. "I don't think God ever intended it to snow down here. I figure he'd leave that mess to you Northerners."

Yvonne laughed as she watched Ted Rappaport hang her coat in the closet. Besides Desmond, he was the only other Rappaport she liked.

"Now where's my hug?" He grabbed Yvonne and gave her a big embrace, then released her. "I like your hair like that," he told her, inspecting it further. Her hair had been swept up and off her face and twisted in several Bantu knots.

"Thank you." Yvonne smiled. "I needed something different."

"Well, it looks nice on you. Desmond seen it yet?"

"Yes, but he doesn't like it as much."

Mr. Rappaport shrugged. "It's going to be a lot of small things like that in a marriage, Yvonne. Don't worry. Anyway, how is my daughter-in-law doing?"

"Future daughter-in-law," Yvonne corrected him. "My last name is still Taylor until November," she teased. The affable aroma of pine wood burning throughout the house pricked at her nostrils.

"Yeah, well, that'll change soon. Everyone is in the family room. Come on in here." Mr. Rappaport motioned with his hand.

Yvonne followed his lead, taking a moment to nod to a

few of the other guests, before making her way down the two steps that led into the knickknack-filled family room. Miles Davis' "Kinda Blue" played in the background, while her eyes continued to search the room for Desmond.

"Yvonne," Mrs. Rappaport sang in her slow, deliberate, quasibourgeois voice. "We were beginning to think you had crashed and burned," she enunciated slowly, still sashaying toward her.

"Yeah, I bet you probably wish it true," Yvonne commented quietly. It had been almost two years, and still Liz Rappaport refused to accept her and Desmond's relationship—even less, engagement. She knew Mrs. Rappaport's feelings, or lack thereof, for her had a lot to do with Desmond's ex-girlfriend, Danni, who had been around for over ten years.

Even after Desmond left Georgia to attend Purdue University, some thousand plus miles across the country, Danni still had managed to keep a brightly lit torch for him. It didn't seem to matter to Danni, or Liz Rappaport for that matter, that Desmond had selected her to be his lifelong companion. Liz Rappaport let it be known to her that her baby boy would be better suited with the very beautiful, exotic-looking Danielle "Danni" Green. Something about with Danni as Desmond's wife, she'd be guaranteed beautiful grandchildren, with *good* hair and *fair* skin.

It had been nineteen months to the day and still not much had changed with regard to Liz Rappaport's attitude or obvious, outward displeasure with me. Except, of course, the fraudulent smile that was now plastered all over her mischievous face. Hearing Liz's haggard tone lulling some more, Yvonne focused back on her current whereabouts.

"What took you so long?" Liz questioned in a jaded tone.

"I had to stop by the office to reorganize some paperwork for one of the partners," Yvonne replied hazily.

"Um-hmm," Liz sarcastically mumbled. "Anyhow," she said dramatically, "you're here now, and I want you to meet a good friend of mine." She paused to nudge the petite, round woman standing next to her. "Doris, this is Desmond's friend, Yvonne. Yvonne, this is my dearest and best friend in the world, Doris."

"Nice to meet you," Yvonne said, extending her hand as her eyes whisked over Doris's physique. A pretty, deep chocolate sister, though a little on the heavy side.

"Same here," Doris said with the same, slow, condescending tone as Liz. Instantly Yvonne knew that Doris's, whatever her last name might be, opinion of her had been tainted by Desmond's mom. "Nice dress," Doris finally acknowledged a few seconds later.

"Thank you." Yvonne batted her eyelashes. The compliment had caught her off guard.

"It's a cute dress. A little out of season for the material and a little big on you. I keep telling Desmond you don't have a childbearing body." Liz gazed at Yvonne's head. "Too busy to do your hair, I see," Liz said, shaking her head, then looking over at Doris.

"Doris here is a judge in Chicago. I told her you were clerking at some tiny firm in Decatur and that you took the bar *again*." She put an emphasis on the word again. "Perhaps she could lend you some pointers on how to land a real position. Once you ever pass the bar."

Just then, and not a minute soon enough, Desmond surfaced from the back of the room. His broad body was cloaked in a bronze tailored suit, offset by a multicolored tie. The dark colored suit accentuated his medium skin tone. Desmond Rappaport wasn't considered a handsome man in particular or an ugly duckling—just an average brother with a great deal of sex appeal. His walk was meaningful and deliberate as he approached Yvonne.

"Here's my fiancée." Desmond grinned, wrapping his arms around Yvonne and planting a sloppy kiss on her perfectly painted lips before easing her away from Doris and his mother. He gave her a quick once over and quietly thought, *She could have at least taken them things out of her head and worn a nice bob for a special occasion like this.*

Gently he squeezed her hand. "This is supposed to be our engagement party, babe. How come you're letting my mother hog all your time?" He smiled teasingly. Hell, he knew there was no love lost between her and his mother.

"Believe me, Desmond. I wasn't trying to have her absorb all my time. I was more intrigued with the fact that Doris is a Superior Court judge in Chicago. That's pretty fascinating even if she is your mom's best friend," she said smugly.

"Really? Well, there are other guests with less elitelike titles waiting to bestow us with congratulatory hugs and gifts. Furthermore, I think we make a damn good tag team ourselves. A lawyer and an engineer. Now that's what I'd call fascinating."

Yvonne's eyes slipped to the back of her head. She didn't laugh at Desmond's intended acclamation. Maybe if Desmond would gather some guts to put his mother in check as opposed to allowing her to run amuck in his personal life, she might be impressed with his being an engineer.

Sensing Yvonne's agitation, Desmond took her hand,

threaded it through his arm, and proudly strolled into the middle of the family room with the rest of the people. They spent the next hour mingling, conversing, and laughing with the other guests, who had strayed throughout the moderate-sized home.

Not a bad turnout, Yvonne thought, as she stood with a glass of cranberry juice in hand. When Desmond first introduced the idea of hosting a quick, informal engagement party at his parents' house, she about gagged. "You want me to believe that your mother is actually supportive of us celebrating our union in her home? Please!" she remembered saying. Desmond shrugged and assured her that everything would work out fine. "Trust me" was how they left off and before long, the party had come to this.

Yvonne took another sip from her glass. She really hadn't had any special requests or requirements, except for one. That Danni Green would chose to keep her glamorous buttocks home and bid congratulations via Southern Bell, the U.S. post office, or any other source other than at their engagement party.

It wasn't jealousy or envy that caused her to negate including Danni as one of the guests for the party. Besides, the few times she had bumped into Danni during the past nineteen months, she appeared to be nice enough. Deep down though, she knew that if Danni had her way, she'd be back in Desmond's life and bed in a twinkling. And no, she didn't feel the least bit afraid of Danielle. Just the thought of trying to handle Danni and Liz Rappaport simultaneously at her engagement party would have been borderline traumatic.

Whenever Yvonne was tempted to feel a twinge of concern about Danni and Desmond's past history, she would just remember what Desmond would often say. He would reassure her that he had gotten the better package deal by selecting her over Danni because not only did she have striking beauty, a strong work ethic, and common sense, but much, much, more brain wattage and usage.

Yvonne spotted her aunt Gigi standing in front of the fireplace, talking with one of her male companions and another couple. Trying to connect eyes with her aunt proved impossible. Aunt Gigi's mouth was busy captivating everyone. Eventually Yvonne captured Aunt Gigi's attention.

Yvonne untangled herself from Desmond's arm, and excused herself from the guest they were entertaining to greet Aunt Gigi, whose welcoming smile was always addictive.

"Aunt Gigiiii." Yvonne smiled while circling around her. "You look mighty elegant. This is a beautiful . . . What is it?" Yvonne pinched the sleeve, attempting to evaluate the material. Forty-nine years old? Hardly, Yvonne protested inwardly, looking over her auntie, who maintained her shapely figure by working out at the gym four times a week. Although Aunt Gigi would often say that the real secret to her youthful look was dating younger men.

"Thank you, baby." Aunt Gigi kissed her niece on the cheek. "It's suede. Got it on sale at Nordstrom's when I was in New York last month. Never mind all that," Gigi said, patting Yvonne's hand. "Look at you. That red dress is stunning on you."

"Funny you should think that 'cause Ms. Liz doesn't seem to share your opinion."

"Ah, who cares about an old, grumpy witch who can't coordinate the basic colors or patterns. I'm here to tell you, you look wonderful, honey. Hair and all." Aunt Gigi placed her arm around Yvonne's waist. "Liz's just mad that you've pried and forever cemented her baby boy's nose open. That's all. Where's that mama's boy at, anyway?"

Yvonne cocked her head toward the opposite side of the room. "He's over there sharing some testosterone stories with his buddies."

"I see," Aunt Gigi replied in a saucy tone. "How old are those fine little friends of his?"

"Same age as Desmond, I think. Except the short one might be thirty-four by now."

"Well, that's only fifteen years or so. It makes no difference once you reach a certain age anyway. If you know what I mean." Aunt Gigi laughed. When Yvonne didn't join her, she asked, "Yvonne, you seem a little down in spirit. Is everything all right?"

Yvonne shrugged. "Yeah. I guess."

"You guess? Honey, this is your engagement party. You're not supposed to be guessing much about anything except how many folks might be standing in this dusty house." Aunt Gigi turned up her nose. "Can you believe it? Hosting a party and not even dusting beforehand. Trifling."

Yvonne nodded her head back and forth. Just like Aunt Gigi to notice minute things like that. Yvonne let her eyes wander past the bookshelf next to the fireplace, spotting a few cobwebs and dust balls etched in the corners of the shelves.

"So . . ." Aunt Gigi said lifting up her drink from the table. "What's the matter with you?"

"When I walked in earlier, I overheard some ladies talking about how much Liz despises me."

"What? Who?"

"Doesn't matter, Auntie. It doesn't change things. Really."

"You know, I've got a good mind to go over there and snatch that wig right off her bald head and let all her so-called friends see what she's really made of."

Yvonne and Aunt Gigi cracked up with laughter, taking a moment of reprieve only when looking up and finding Desmond standing before them.

"Hello, Aunt Gigi," Desmond uttered before placing a kiss on her cheek. "What's so funny?" He really didn't have to ask. He was certain it was an inside joke, probably at the expense of his mother. Desmond exhaled a deep breath. He really did wish that Yvonne and his mother could get along much better. But he knew that would be impossible for two reasons: one, just because; two, Danni Green.

Danni, Danni, Danni—that's all his mother talked about, and truthfully speaking, Danni seemed to be all that was on his mind of late, too. The stroke of Aunt Gigi's hand against his jacket shook his mind free from his muse.

"Desmond, your friends sure are handsome. Are they engineers as well?" Aunt Gigi inquired.

"No, ma'am. Rick plays for the Falcons, and Reggie is finishing his last year of residency."

"Really?" Aunt Gigi said, sipping on her straw again. "Perhaps you'll introduce me before I leave."

"Sure thing, Aunt Gigi." Desmond chuckled. "But right now we need to cut the cake and honor a few toasts. You ready, sweetheart?" Desmond said, looking at Yvonne. He didn't wait for a reply. He simply grabbed Yvonne by the hand and led her back across the room toward the rectangular table, which was topped with a one-layer strawberry sheet cake, with *Congrats!* written on it in blue icing and surrounded by several gift boxes.

Desmond's father invited all the guests to make their

way around the table so that they could toast Yvonne and Desmond. The people bustled around for a few minutes more before everyone secured a spot around the table, forming a fairly closed circle. The loud voices had simmered down to a murmur before Ted Rappaport turned down the volume to Al Green's "Joy & Happiness." Liz Rappaport stood a few feet behind him, holding a mixed cocktail in her hand and a strained smile on her face.

Mr. Rappaport cleared his throat before saying, "Ladies and gentlemen, at this time my wife, Liz, and I would like to thank you for coming out, in less than desirable weather, to help us congratulate our son, Desmond, and his fiancée, Yvonne, on their engagement. Come on over here, you two," he said, waving them to move closer. A few more seconds elapsed before Desmond and Yvonne stood directly to the left of Mr. Rappaport.

"It is during times like this that we are happy to see that young folks still believe in the importance and sacred writ of marriage."

"Hear ye," Liz joined in while the guests cluttered the room with thick, clapping sounds over the soft music in the background. She continued, "I would just like to say that the only thing I wish for as Desmond's mother is his *true* happiness." The clapping resumed again, only louder.

In fact, the praising was so loud that no one recognized the rumbling noises of items being tossed over. It wasn't until the clapping died down to barely a tap that the loud, clashing sounds became more audible. At once, everyone turned around to view who was responsible for making such a ruckus. As the crowd began to step apart, causing the circle to now become a horseshoe, with the opening toward the back of the room, the tall, staggering female figure came more into focus.

"I don't believe this," Yvonne spewed angrily. "What is she doing here?"

"Heeeey, that's right. It's the long-lost Danni," the mystery woman slurred. "Did I hear something about you wishing for Desmond's true happiness, Mrs. Rappaport?" she said, walking closer to the head of the table where Desmond stood with his eyes wide and alarmed—Yvonne, with rage swelling her cheeks.

Yvonne shot a piercing glance at Liz, then she flicked a cold glare at the gorgeous Danni. The room fell completely silent—conversation and laughter ceased—Najee's saxophone halted. God, Yvonne thought. It was like one of those special broadcast sirens had gone off, and everybody was waiting for the announcement.

"I thought I'd drop by and pay my *rezspects*. Nobody bothered to send me an invitation, so's I has to invites myself, I guess." Obviously Danni had had too many glasses of gin and juice. There was no other reason for her behavior.

"Don't let me stop ya'll. Go on with what you were about to say about this oh so amazing couple." Danni snickered, stumbling over to the side slightly. "And while ya'll at it, try and find out the secret as to why Desmond couldn't find me so amazing enough to marry. Hell, we all know I amaze him in bed. But not enough for him to marry? Come, come now."

"Danni," Desmond said, hurriedly walking toward her. "You're drunk. You need to go home and sleep it off."

Liz Rappaport had quickly gone to Danni's rescue as well. "Desmond, can't you see she can't drive in this condition?"

"Well, she got here fine enough, didn't she, Mother?"

"Oh, Desmond, chill out. I took a cab. Do you really

think I'd be so stupid as to down a half bottle of Jack Daniel's, then get behind my wheel? Pleeze."

"Come on, Danni, let's get you upstairs now and lie you down," Mrs. Rappaport insisted, tugging on her arm slightly.

"Naw, I'm all right, Liz. Quit pulling on my threads," she said, yanking her arm free. "I just came by to give Desmond his gift. That's all."

Yvonne's face was flushed with hot blood as she sauntered across the room toward the ghastly looking woman, who had obviously come to ruin her party. Stopping only about a foot away from Danni, and only after Desmond wedged his body between the two women, Yvonne shot Danni a death-wish look and snarled, "Danni, just exactly what kind of gift do you have to give to Desmond?"

Danni stared at Yvonne for a long minute, then burst out with a loud, calculating laugh. "What kind of gift do I have for him? Let's just say it's one you can't give him right now."

"Really? Seems to me the only one that came here empty handed and headed is you. The only gift you could possibly give at this time is a farewell one. You know what I mean?"

"You still don't get it, do you, Yvonne? I'm not going a damn place and haven't in almost ten years. Matter of fact, if there is going to be a farewell tune, you'll be the one humming it."

"Okay, ladies. That's enough," Mr. Rappaport warned, stepping in between Desmond and Danni. "Danni, what is it you want to give to Desmond so I can take you home."

Danni stared at Mr. Rappaport for some time, wondering for a moment if he ever did like her. Don't matter now, she dismissed silently before looking over at Liz, then Yvonne, before resting her eyes on Desmond.

Danni let a slow smile creep across her face, then ran her left hand across her belly before singing, *"A son."*

Yvonne shot a jarring glare at Desmond. She searched his face and body language, needing to get a sense of the situation. Desmond stood slouching, while fidgeting fingers ran through the collar of his shirt. His eyes wide and averting—his nutmeg-colored face drained of its color. His hesitation and unwillingness to immediately deny the accusation rendered the painful confirmation Yvonne dreaded. By everything she could tell about her so-called prince charming, Desmond Rappaport had definitely fathered Danni Green with a baby.

Two

And so Yvonne Taylor stood, shocked, befuddled, and dangerously angry in the middle of the Rappaports' home, with about twenty or so open mouths, at Danni's startling news. Had it not been for Aunt Gigi, who quickly summoned her friend, grabbed her coat and purse, and led her niece out of the chaotic pit, Yvonne wasn't sure she would have made it through the scenario. She had restrained her desire to slap Desmond. Had even retarded her urge to cry through the initial news and through Desmond's pressured admittance of sleeping with Danni, until she got into the car.

Aunt Gigi, who never incorporated profanity into her vocabulary, had done nothing but use all the familiar cuss words as she drove aggressively and cursed Desmond aloud. She had worked herself up so much that she even threatened to kick Liz's butt the next time she saw her. This bought a much needed spurt of laughter from Yvonne, who visualized her aunt Gigi, with her salt-and-pepper hair, wedging her size tens between the crack of Mrs. Rappaport's particular anatomy.

The immediate days following the devastating scenario were very difficult and painful for Yvonne. She refused to go to the office because there was no way she felt up to facing her co-workers. She stayed in the bed and got out of it only to use the bathroom or get something to drink. Her appetite had diminished, and she had purposely ignored the telephone's beckoning as well as the doorbell.

But Aunt Gigi's determination not to let her niece get too far down into a blue funk finally paid off. After a week of ducking and dodging the world, Yvonne resurfaced. Barely. Everyone at the law firm had been more than supportive, ensuring that they said or did nothing that reminded her of Desmond or the painful breakup. They had even gone so far as to change the radio station from the familiar quiet storm format, known for its love ballads, to a more hip, upbeat one.

Desmond attempted to plead his side of the story, saying something about his forsaking Yvonne with Danni was a deeply regretted mistake. And that Danni had seduced him after he had had too many drinks one night while out with some friends and while Yvonne was home studying for the bar.

As if studying for the bar really had anything to do with his actions, Yvonne had snapped at Desmond. Like she told him, it was bad enough that he slept with Danni to begin with, but to do it on more than one occasion and create a child? That would never be forgiven.

As the days progressed, Yvonne thanked everyone at her office for their support and effort in trying to keep her feelings protected. The throb regarding her breakup with Desmond seemed unbearable at times. Always bumping into people and going places that reminded her of their relationship was nerve-wracking. She would withstand the pain and uneasiness as long as she could. She didn't want to cut off everyone that she and Desmond knew and shared a mutual friendship with. But if things got too crazy, *pow-dow!* Off she would go.

As it was, she could hardly chin up when she saw some of Desmond's fraternity brothers the other day at the grocery store. Now, as she stood peering at the eight-and-a-half-by-eleven piece of white paper with the unique watermark in the shadows, she knew it was time to make a change.

Damn! She had failed the Georgia State Bar a third time. She crumbled the piece of paper into a ball. Perhaps Aunt Gigi's suggestion that she get away for a while wasn't such a bad idea. She'd discuss it with Aunt Gigi over dinner tomorrow night. But first, she needed to find her phone book and place a phone call. There was someplace she could escape to after all.

When Aunt Gigi arrived at Yvonne's apartment the next evening, Yvonne had already come to a decision. Los Angeles, California, would serve as her new abode for an undisclosed period of time. She would relocate to the West Coast and stay with her cousin, Adrianne, until she figured out what she was going to do next with her life: continue to teach dance classes to underprivileged children on the side? or take the bar a fourth time?

Aunt Gigi sat at the table, motionless at the mention of Yvonne's plans. Good grief, she fussed silently. She wanted Yvonne to get away but not way the hell across the country.

"Adrianne?" Aunt Gigi finally voiced, dropping her salad fork into the wooden bowl. "Isn't that your crazy cousin on your mom's side of the family? What in the world would you want to do that for?"

"Oh, Aunt Gigi, Adrianne and I go way back. She's all right. A little out to the left but okay overall. We attended college together. Anyway, I was speaking with her yesterday and briefly filling her in on what happened. She told me to come on out. She has a three-bedroom town house, and one of those rooms has my name on it." Yvonne removed Aunt Gigi's empty plate from the table.

"How can she afford a three-bedroom home in Los Angeles by herself." Aunt Gigi asked, leaning back in the chair. "She's not dealing with the wrong kind of folks, is she?"

"No," Yvonne mumbled softly. "She's a CPA with her own business. Adrianne has always been geared for success." She was scraping the excess food off the plates and shoving it down the garbage disposal.

Aunt Gigi took a moment to digest the information before replying, "If my memory serves me correctly, didn't you and Adrianne have some kind of falling out about some guy when you were in college?"

"That was a long time ago. It's all water under the bridge now. Anyway . . ." Yvonne paused, shaking the excess water off her hands. "I mentioned my going to L.A. to Douglass, one of the partners at the firm, and he told me he has a good friend who is a partner at a medium-sized firm in L.A. He's going to talk to him and find out what's happening. Maybe things will fall into place for me there."

"Are you planning to drive or fly?"

"Fly. I'll send for my car later—once I get to know the place—decide if I'm going to become a permanent resident."

"I see." Aunt Gigi gave her niece a leveled gaze, then asked, "What are you going to do about your dancing stuff?"

"I'll find a group of disadvantaged youths in Los Angeles to volunteer my gift with. There's so many children out here who could benefit from dancing. I'll find a good church home or organization that will lend me the space to teach my classes."

"How much money you got saved to take with you?"

"Close to two thousand dollars. It was mostly going to help pay for the . . ." Yvonne's heart dropped again. She couldn't even bring herself to say the word *wedding*. It was like the word had done something awful to her, when instead she knew it was all Desmond and that damn Danni's doing.

Aunt Gigi, sensing Yvonne's relapse, quickly came to the rescue. "That's not a whole lot of money, Yvonne, when you're talking about relocating across the United States, no matter how temporary it may be. You've got your car payment and student loans and credit cards and . . ."

Aunt Gigi paused. She was beginning to sound more like she was raining on Yvonne's parade than supporting it. Aunt Gigi smiled softly. "You do what's best for you, sugar. I'll try to help you the best way I can."

Yvonne placed a gentle hand on her auntie. It was nice of her to offer, but she also knew Aunt Gigi didn't have the extra money to spare. Not with the way all her assets were being tied up in her nasty divorce proceedings.

"I'll be fine, Aunt Gi. Don't worry." Yvonne patted her hand again. "I could sell my ring. I should be able to get a thousand dollars for it at least."

"That's all that ring is worth?" Aunt Gigi scoffed. "Cheap son of a—"

Yvonne laughed. "I'll swing by the jewelers first thing in the morning and have him look at it. It'll all work out,

Aunt Gigi. Nothing could go much worse than it has for me here in this fine state we know and love as Georgia," Yvonne mimicked in her best rendition of a southern belle drawl.

The only other real issue at heart was the sixty-five hundred dollars she had let Desmond talk her into charging on her American Express gold card for a family boat. A boat that they were supposed to use for their fishing expeditions, a boat that Desmond currently held in his possession, a boat whose title papers were in his name.

Yvonne let out a frustrated breath. Not to worry. There was no way Desmond would jeopardize her good credit rating behind this. As soon as Desmond received the money from his share options he cashed in next month, he would certainly write her a check. She trusted him.

"So, Aunt Gigi," Yvonne said after a few minutes. "Knowing everything will be okay, will I leave here with your blessing or not?"

Aunt Gigi placed her hands on her hips and smiled so widely that the silver-colored fillings in the back of her teeth were showing. "Of course, baby. Of course."

The next morning, Yvonne began making preparations to relocate across country. It would be a test of strength, she knew, but well worth it. In a new place such as L.A., no one knew her or the pain she suffered, except for Adrianne. She was going to be free to be whoever or whatever type of person she desired to be: dancer, lawyer, or both.

She would forge new friendships and reevaluate her life goals and endeavors. The idea of starting over fresh in a new place was exhilarating. The feeling of excitement was probably similar to what a witness protection candidate must have felt when they were given a second chance. Truthfully speaking, Los Angeles had been the only thing she could lean on to make her smile—get through the days.

Beneath the pain, Yvonne feared two things. One, that she would never find anyone to love her enough again to make a true commitment. Two, she would never trust someone enough to be open to making a commitment. *Damn Desmond Rappaport.* Yvonne frowned.

The phone rang loudly. Yvonne flinched. She had drifted off into some ill thoughts about Desmond and Danni. She walked through a herd of duct-taped boxes toward the phone, turning down the ringer once she lifted the receiver.

"Hello," she said in a voice sounding like morning hoarseness, her voice obviously at a resting state for too long. She moved the receiver upward on an angle—away from her mouth, and cleared her throat.

Silence settled on the other end of the phone line. Yvonne greeted the would-be caller again. "Hello?" she said a little more forcefully this time.

The line remained airy. Yvonne swore she heard what sounded like strained breathing on the other end. *Irritating.* She clicked the phone back down in its cradle, but decided to leave the receiver off the hook instead. This was the fifth time in a three-day period that the crank caller had phoned. No doubt in her mind—it was probably Danielle Green.

Yvonne labeled the last two boxes with the black magic marker. She'd leave most of her things in Aunt Gigi's garage until she figured out what her permanent zip code was going to be. *Los Angeles, California. Unbelievable. And all by my lonesome. Uhmp. Who would have thought?* She swiped her forehead with a paper towel, then sat down atop of one of the boxes. She let out a heavy sigh. This trip to Los Angeles was exactly what she needed at this point in her life. Exactly.

Days of crying and sniffling, packing and taping, storing and shipping boxes were finished. D-day had finally arrived. Aunt Gigi pulled in front of the departure area at Hartsfield Airport in Atlanta, where she prepared herself to bid Yvonne a warm farewell. She used her chiropractor appointment as an excuse not to walk Yvonne down to her gate.

All week long, Aunt Gigi had rehearsed the goodbye. She had done her best to treat Yvonne's departure like an extended business trip. This psychological ploy worked for a while until Yvonne's eyes filled with tears. She reached over and kissed Yvonne on the cheek, then gave her a tight hug.

"I'll see you when you get back from your trip." Aunt Gigi brushed the side of her face. "And you can meet me right here, too."

Yvonne wiped beneath her eyes as she watched the brake lights to Aunt Gigi's Volvo merge in with the rest of the traffic. The tall brother at the curbside check-in came over and picked up her luggage.

"Where to?" he said, dropping the pieces of luggage on the ground again.

"Los Angeles," Yvonne said, searching for her plane ticket.

"Been to L.A. before?"

"This is a first." Yvonne handed him the ticket. "Have you been there before?"

"Sure have," the brother replied, continuing to clip the

tags onto her bags. "Didn't care for it one bit. People there are too phony for me. I suppose it'll be okay for you young folks. But for me, give me a southern woman any day." He smiled and handed Yvonne her ticket.

Yvonne flashed a tight grin and took the ticket from the elderly gent with the silver hair.

"Thank you," she said, handing him three dollars. Really, she could care less about an L.A. woman or man. She was not going there to find her a man. Nor was she in the mood to deal with any men at this point in her life. This L.A. trip was simply to get away—to figure things out. That's all.

"You're welcome, miss. Your gate number is thirty-three, and you're due to start boarding in about an hour. Have a good trip. And stay away from them producer types," the skycap said, looking up suddenly with an arched brow. "Every damn man out there, black or white, claims to be a producer or something. Just keep your wits about ya."

Yvonne responded with a nod in the affirmative. She pushed her hands into the pockets of her jeans to loosen them up. She should have chosen a less fitted blouse, one that didn't require tucking in. Tossing the medium-sized, plaid duffel bag onto her shoulder, she made her way downstairs to the trains. Gate C was where she stepped off the light rail and took the high inclined escalator up to the top level.

Walking toward her gate, Yvonne took a minute to stop in and browse the magazine section of a gift shop. Feeling someone looking her over, she lifted up her head and was stunned to notice a very handsome brother, with a brighter than necessary smile, staring at her. Yvonne's immediate reaction was to turn away. And she did—but not before

connecting eyes with the tall gentleman for five or six
seconds.

The strange man's flirtatious smile and designer cologne
skewed her thoughts. Definitely not the trustworthy type.
She hadn't wanted to glance back up at him again but she
did. And she shouldn't have done that because now the
brother with the full lips had uttered a bewitching hello.

Yvonne's jaws locked. It was apparent that this brother
wanted to indulge in more friendly conversation, but she
was not the tiniest bit interested. Shyly she acknowledged
his greeting with a trite head nod, plucked the magazines
of her choice, and raced to the cashier line. *Maybe during
another time, brotherman, because I'm not interested in
flirting with you or any other man at this time in my life.*

Six hours. That's a long time to be stuck in the air with
complete strangers, Yvonne fretted, finding a seat in the
gate area. She dropped the bag on the gray carpet and sat
down on the hard, blue plastic seat. Quickly she scanned
the area, trying to consider her traveling companions. She
slipped the earphones to her portable CD player over her
ears. The smooth sounds of "Blackstreet" caressed her
mind as she flipped through the first magazine, stopping
often between articles to observe the seating area.

Thirty or forty minutes had elapsed before she looked
up again and noticed a line forming at the ticket counter.
Rising slowly, so as not to drop her CD player, which lay
in her lap, Yvonne slid the headphones down around her
neck, held the CD player in her left hand, and stood at the
end of the line.

"I can help you here, ma'am," the tall, blond woman
smiled, waving her over to the left side of the ticket counter.

Yvonne greeted the agent with the same welcoming
smile and handed her the ticket.

"Okay, Ms. Taylor. We have you assigned to aisle eight, seat B. It's a window seat like you requested. We'll be boarding in a few more minutes."

"Thanks," Yvonne said, taking her ticket from the agent and then sitting back down in her seat. The waiting area had become more crowded with people standing against the columns and sitting on their luggage. She draped her earphones over her head again.

Good Lord, all these people are going to L.A.? Must be something right going on there, she thought, looking at her watch. Sure hope we can get out of here on time. And I hope Adrianne has good enough sense to call the airport before she goes out there.

Yvonne turned down the volume to the CD player, closed the magazine, and watched as the people with seats in the higher-number rows began boarding the plane. She felt a twinge of uncertainty come over her when she heard the agent announce her row. *This is it,* she determined silently, while standing and gathering her things. She let out a deep, nervous breath. *I can't believe I'm actually doing this.*

Suddenly she felt that familiar lump in her throat resurfacing again. Desperately she wanted to let it go. But she fought back the urge, as she had done off and on for so many days now. Why the heck was she going way across country again? she wondered for the thirtieth time. *To start anew—start over fresh.* She reached up and placed her overnight bag in the overhead compartment.

Her hands were clammy and cold. Her heart beat to its own rhythm as she stared out the window, watching the bag handlers load the bottom of the plane with loads of luggage. Small drops of rain were beginning to sprinkle downward as were the tears from her eyes. *To get a grip on my life choices and objectives. That's why,* she rehearsed inwardly, wiping her eyes.

She felt someone towering above her but chose not to look, at least not until she could pull her emotions together. Probably just the passenger seated next to her. More than likely, with her luck, it was some old, self-centered, blabbermouth who would talk her ear off the entire flight.

She continued to stare out the window, feeling the weight of her seat shift as the passenger next to her had obviously taken his seat. The pleasant scent of a man's cologne whisked past her nostrils. Unconsciously she sniffed again to inhale more of the heavy aroma. Still fixated on the baggage handlers outside the window, Yvonne could hear the flight attendant going up and down the aisle, clamping shut the overhead compartments. The clicking noise stopped abruptly when she reached her row, as the female attendant addressed the person sitting next to her.

"Sir, would you like for me to place that bag in an overhead compartment for you? It's too big to be considered an under-the-seat item."

"I'll do it if you'd like," he said in a smooth tone. "I couldn't find any space for it other than under my seat."

Yvonne felt her seat shift once again when the passenger stood up. Her heartbeat quickened at the thought that the man sitting next to her was more than likely a brother. She could tell by his voice and the way he pronounced the word *do,* with an emphasis on the *ooh* part of the word, that he was a Northerner. Well, at least he smelled good, she thought, slyly wiping away any telltale signs of smeared mascara from under her eyes.

There was some sort of a tussle in the overhead compartment for a while as the flight attendant and her seat companion struggled to squeeze his bag in with the rest of the luggage pieces.

"Perhaps if we remove some of these pillows and blankets, your bag might fit yet," the attendant mumbled. "Ma'am," she said unexpectedly, catching Yvonne off guard. "Would you care for a pillow or a blanket?"

Yvonne turned her head slowly to greet the attendant, not knowing if she wanted to come face to face with Mr. Aromatic.

"Sure," Yvonne bashfully replied, taking the pillow and blanket from the woman. "Thank you." She flashed a perky smile before letting her eyes shift toward the tall, athletically built man, whom she had seen earlier in the gift shop. Their eyes locked again briefly before the brother passed a *well, well, well* smile at Yvonne.

This time she matched his shining smile, then slowly unglued her gaze and shifted it down to her lap where she searched for her other seat belt strap. Great. Just my luck, she sighed. She only hoped that he was not the talkative sort. Didn't matter no how because she had her CD player and her magazines to keep her otherwise engaged.

"What about you, sir? Would you care for a pillow?" the attendant questioned.

"Yes, I would. Thank you," he said, sitting down in his seat, causing Yvonne's chair to shift again.

"Here you go," he said, holding on to Yvonne's other seat belt. "These things always get tangled up."

"Yes, I see," she said coolly, taking the belt from him. "Thanks."

"You're welcome." He hesitated before continuing. "Seems like the people who clean these planes purposely tie up the seat belts just to test a passenger's patience. As if the flight itself isn't challenging enough."

Yvonne didn't respond. She simply fastened her seat belt and focused back out the window. She didn't want to get into any type of discussion with this brother—no matter how fine he was and no matter how articulate he sounded, with his proper-speaking self.

"Sean," he said gleefully, extending his right hand. He sensed her hesitation but was beside himself. Silently he thanked God that he had insisted on having changed to an aisle seat so that he could stretch out his lanky legs.

Yvonne stared at his enormous hand before reluctantly cupping it. "Yvonne," she replied even more aloofly. The warmth and softness of his hand wrapped around hers made her want to dawdle in the handshake. She felt the magnetism instantly. As if she had been dragging her feet across the carpet, then touched a metal lamp. The spark was alarming at first. But the longer their hands lingered together, the less she felt threatened. Delicately she withdrew her hand.

"Beautiful name, Yvonne. I'll have to tell my sister there's another name to consider for the baby if it's a girl." He smiled.

"How sweet," she replied matter-of-factly, looking him in the eyes. Something sensuous about his eyes and those daggone bushy brows. She could already tell that this guy was going to be a thorn in her side. He seemed hell-bent on stirring up a conversation with her. Yvonne let loose a deep slow breath before turning her head toward the window again.

Sean babbled on. "I think she's due in two or three months. I'm not really sure. One thing I do know is that my brother in-law is hoping for a son. Figures, huh? Most brothers want a son first. Personally I'd rather have a little girl first."

Realizing that Sean was going to yap on and on until she indulged him, Yvonne took one final look out the window. The baggage handlers were done loading the plane anyway. Rolling her eyes toward the back of her head, something she did whenever she felt bothered or uncomfortable, or obligated, she replied, "Really? Why is that?"

"Because when my wife gets mad with me, I can still count on the unconditional love of Daddy's little girl." He grinned.

Yvonne smiled dutifully. What was it about her that compelled this brother to keeping talking? If he were the perceptive type of man, he would have figured by now that she wasn't in the mood for small chitchat. That she had had a very jacked-up couple of weeks; that her heart and mind were someplace else.

Sean gave Yvonne a swift once-over. Yvonne was a very attractive woman. She had her hair twisted in one of those ethnic styles he had seen featured on the front cover of *Essence* magazine and that he liked so much. *Very nice.* His eyes roved downward. There was no sign of a wedding ring or engagement ring, which made him even more comfortable.

Her unwillingness to offer more than one or two sentences told him she was either reserved, preoccupied, or mending from a torn heart. Something about this mahogany colored sister made him want to help her relax, open up—at least while she was in his presence. Choosing not to let her aloofness get the best of him, Sean proceeded with a question.

"Do you have any children, Yvonne?"

"No," she replied curtly. Good Lord, he's just not going to get the hint, is he? Irritated she shifted her left ankle across her right.

"Something I said?" Sean asked, detecting the roughness in her voice and sudden body change.

"You just don't give up, do you?" she asked, eyeing him again.

Sean hesitated. Was he really being that overbearing? Not really, he decided. He searched her face for a few seconds more, really wishing he had a full face-to-face view of her.

Contemplating his answer, he responded, "Not when I see people hurting." He knew he was reaching—but, oh well. If she was unhappy with his forwardness, he was sure she would have no problem telling him so.

Yvonne quietly turned away, looking straight ahead and honing in on the flight attendant, who was walking down the aisle counting the passengers. Guess he was more perceptive than she had given him credit for. Well, what was it to him if she was in pain. . . . There was nothing he could do to make it all better anyway. She let out a deep breath. Perhaps she was being somewhat difficult, not to mention unfriendly.

She decided she would cut Sean some slack. Besides, he wasn't the reason for her disposition. Desmond Rappaport and Danni Green were. She shifted her leg again, then asked, "What about you, Sean? You have any children?"

"No, ma'am," Sean replied, startled. "I can honestly say that God hasn't blessed me with any little ones yet. I'm sure he'd want me to be around to raise my children. I don't suppose I'll be fathering any kids until I get married one day."

The flight attendant's voice over the PA cut off their conversation—a clear signal that they were ready for take-off. Yvonne checked the tightness of her seat belt once more, then transferred her attention toward the front of the plane. For the next two minutes or so, Yvonne absently absorbed the flight attendant's rhetoric.

She was well acquainted with the survival procedures in the unlikely event of an emergency and the plane went down. She couldn't count the numerous flights she had taken from North Carolina to New Jersey while getting her undergraduate degree in Greensboro. Nothing had changed but the length of the flights once she moved to Atlanta to attend the University of Georgia law school. She had racked up so many Frequent-Flyer miles over the many years that she was able to cash them in twice for a trip to the Bahamas and Puerto Rico.

The airborne sensation caused Yvonne's stomach to drop a bit. She was used to flying but always dreaded take-offs. She let her head rest against the back of her seat, attempting to control the queasy feeling arising inside her. A few minutes later, the plane leveled off and Yvonne was relieved. She glanced over at Sean, who didn't seem the least bit bothered by the lift-off. She wondered how many flights he had taken in his lifetime. Yvonne silently paged through her second magazine, quietly wishing that Sean would choose not to start their conversation again.

Having noticed Yvonne engrossed in her magazine, Sean became preoccupied with his own reading material, although deep down he'd much rather prefer to continue the dialogue with the lovely lady sitting to his right. After thumbing through a few pages of his paperwork, Sean let out a yawn. No way could this boring technical reading be as stimulating as the dialogue with Yvonne.

"The good thing about going west is we'll gain three hours. I sure could use them." Sean yawned again. "Do you live in L.A. or are you visiting?"

Yvonne kept her thumb on the page, before shutting the magazine. What is it going to take to shut this brother up? She let out a weary breath. Might as well make the best of it, she decided before replying, "Relocating. Temporarily."

"Really? That's uncommon. Usually most people are trying to leave the city of lost angels. You must be in the entertainment business because you have that model-slash-actress look."

Yvonne let out a hearty chuckle before saying, "Hardly. Thank you for the compliment, but fortunately I have no desire to become an actress. I just need a change. That's all."

Sean looked Yvonne over again. She sure is a pretty sister. I can't believe someone would just let her take off like this and move clear across the United States without putting up some kind of a fuss, he thought. "Somebody special must be waiting for your arrival in Los Angeles, because I can't imagine someone in Atlanta letting you slip away."

Yvonne's cheeks flushed with blood again, she was sure. Had she been one of these light-skinned sisters, it would have been obvious to Sean that he was making her blush.

"Yeah." She grinned at the thought. "There's someone special waiting for me all right. My cousin, Adrianne. The only person I know in L.A." She was loosening up some now. "She invited me out to stay with her until I pull myself together." Oops, that was a slip, she scolded herself. She had no intention of giving Sean the indication that she was unstable or irresponsible.

He knew it. Sean had discerned the pain hidden behind those oval eyes. He sensed her further discomfort as soon as she let the sentence roll out of her mouth. Her body language told him so as she shifted the position of her ankles again.

Obviously there was a grievous reason for Yvonne wanting to relocate to L.A. just as he had thought. There had to be, Sean reasoned to himself. How many people would want to give up the progressiveness and affordability of Atlanta to move to a city well on its way to destruction if they weren't seeking Hollywood dreams?

"It's his loss," Sean whispered. He was taking another stab in the dark here, he knew. But what the heck—it wasn't like he had anywhere to go for the next six hours, and he had a gut feeling that she needed to open up and talk. By the surprised look on Yvonne's face, Sean was sure he struck a nerve.

Dang it, she murmured inwardly. Apparently her pain was still obvious. She sighed. She really wanted to be over that entire dreadful experience with Desmond and Danni. Four weeks had hardly been enough time for her to be considered on the road to wellness again. Even the move to California was like slapping a Band-Aid on a wound that hadn't finished bleeding. Perhaps sharing her story instead of burying it would be cleansing. Okay, she decided, *I'll share my story with Mr. Smell Good.*

"I was engaged to be married," Yvonne began. "During our engagement party, his ex-girlfriend crashed the party claiming that she had a gift for him. And do you know what that gift was, Sean?"

Sean shook his head no but didn't open his mouth. Yvonne was sharing now, and he didn't want to jeopardize that by making any comments.

Yvonne took a deep breath. Reliving the experience was hurtful. Feeling the familiar set of emotions stirring in her soul, she uttered, "A son."

An hour later, Sean was soothingly stroking the top of Yvonne's hand, while she told her story through sometimes teary eyes. Yvonne had already saturated his hanky, which he always kept in his inner jacket pocket. Or in the case like today, in the inside pocket of his vest.

"Sometimes, Yvonne, these things happen to us," Sean said softly, still caressing her hand. "We can't reason it or rationalize it away—much less avoid the deep pain it causes. God has his own agenda for why we are faced with certain situations. We may not know the reason at the time, but given a few months or even a few years, we'll see why he's allowed us to be denied certain people or things.

"I know you've probably heard all this before," Sean went on saying to her. "But it's better that you found out about this Desmond character and his indiscretions before you married him. What if after your honeymoon you found out? What if you were pregnant with his child, too? Then what? You could be in more pain than you are now. Right?" Sean waved his hand. "Forget him."

"I suppose so, Sean." Yvonne sniffled. "I just never expected to have something like this happen to me. You hear about it all the time on those talk shows." She chuckled nervously. "I just thought things were different with me and Desmond. I thought he was a different kind of man."

"Just know that it's not like that with all brothers. Keep an open mind even if your heart is closed right now, okay?"

"Humph." She smiled. "I'll try."

"Good, because you never know when something positive might be lurking around the corner for you one day," Sean said with a raised brow.

"Is that right?"

"Um-hmm." He grinned assuredly. "There's more

good, wholesome, plump fish in the sea. Whenever you're ready, you just have to throw out the line. The real fish will not be afraid to be chummed. You'll see."

Yvonne stared at Sean in bewilderment. What did he know? How could he be so sure, so confident about her emotions? She sighed heavily. Apparently God had purposely chartered their paths, ensuring their fate in meeting today. Sean's gleaming smile, and genuine stroking voice of concern, made it all the more comfortable for her to open up to him.

Since Sean had coerced her to open up and share about her life, now would be a good time to find out about his life. Calming down from her emotional outbreak, she asked, "What about you, Sean? Anyone special in your life?"

"No, not before this moment," he joshed. "L.A. women don't do it for me."

"You don't date occasionally?"

"Sometimes I come across a decent woman at the grocery store, at the cleaners, or on an airplane." He smiled wider. Yvonne grinned helplessly. "Actually I'm tired of the whole dating experience. I don't look forward to doing all that interviewing and pretending and getting-to-know-you part of it. It can be a draining experience."

"I can imagine. I'm not looking forward to getting back in the dating scene, either," Yvonne said, shaking her head.

"Well, when you are ready to test the waters again, you be sure to let me be the first to know. I promise I won't jump up and bite you," he said, gnashing his teeth together playfully.

There it was again. That electric gaze between them. Sean never let his eyes wander away from Yvonne's eyes until the flight attendant approached their seats to offer them drinks.

"What would you like to drink, ma'am?" the flight attendant asked.

"Apple juice, please," Yvonne replied.

"And you, sir?"

"I'll have the same, please."

The attendant handed them their drinks and a bag of peanuts before asking, "We will be serving meat loaf or chicken for dinner—what would you prefer?"

"Chicken for me," Yvonne replied.

"I'll have the chicken, too," Sean responded. He waited a few seconds until the flight attendant was no longer in earshot and teased, "Meat loaf? Can you imagine what that would taste like? I knew I should have let my grandmother pack me a plate. But nooo, I had to be so Mr. Independent. It's not like I do a whole lot of cooking while I'm in L.A."

Yvonne liked the fact that Sean was able to poke fun at himself. It was a trait she didn't find too often in men. Well, at least not in Desmond. He was too immersed in keeping up his image, like his mama. She shook her head after realizing she had let Desmond creep into her mind again. "How long have you lived in California?"

"Three and a half years. Can't stand the place, either," he said, turning up his nose. "It's a septic tank full of mistrust, lies, drugs, and whatever else you can think of."

"If you hate it so much, why are you there? Are you sure there's no one special keeping you there?" Yvonne's mistrust in men caused her to ask the question a second time.

"A California babe? I told you, hardly likely."

"Then why are you there? Sounds like you'd rather be in Atlanta."

"My job sent me there for a four-year stint. I've got six months to go, then I'm o-u-t.," he said, waving his left hand. "Out, out, out."

"What do you do?"

"I'm, uh, an airplane mechanic of sorts," he stammered. "I landed a job that has me situated in America's armpit."

"Come on, Sean. L.A. can't be that bad. Can it?"

Sean saw the concern in Yvonne's eyes and remembered the reason why she was moving to L.A. to begin with. Not wanting to dampen her spirits, he tried to lighten up the conversation. "You're right." He exhaled. "I suppose L.A. has its good points, too. For example, there's plenty of nightlife. And you can always get tickets to a studio taping of the hottest shows. Maybe it's not all bad."

"Liar." Yvonne laughed loudly.

Sean joined in with the chuckling, mainly because he found her forthrightness refreshing and her calling him a liar hysterical. Although he knew he wasn't a liar, but in this instance he was misrepresenting his true feelings about L.A. for the sake of keeping her feeling good about her decision to relocate. And hopefully keeping her feeling good about spending more time with him once she got settled in the area. It had been a long time since he felt this moved by a woman. Probably had a lot to do with the fact that she wasn't tainted with Los Angeles ways. At least not yet.

"God, this is a long flight," Yvonne said, shifting in her seat.

"Come on now, Yvonne. Six hours in the sky isn't really all that bad if you're seated next to the right person." Sean grinned enticingly. Yvonne's cheeks flushed again. "Now you know two people in L.A.: me and your cousin. It won't be so bad. Trust me," he said, stroking her chin lightly, then picking up her hand.

Yvonne felt a familiar chill shiver her body at his touch. "I thought you said L.A. was the land of mistrust. Why would I trust you?" she whispered. She had no intention of trusting him or any other man in her life at this time.

" 'Cause, one"—he paused to move a little closer to her until his sweet, apple-flavored breath fanned her nostrils—"I'm not from L.A. And two, I know that I would never do anything to hurt a beautiful sister like you."

Three

Yvonne yawned for the third time right in the middle of her and Sean's conversation. They had been flying for three and a half hours already and talking for a good bit of that time. She could feel her eyes beginning to droop.

"Why don't you close those pretty little eyes of yours and get some sleep?" Sean said gently.

"I'm okay, Sean," Yvonne said, reaching above and turning off the air vent before draping the blanket over her.

"Now who's lying?" He smiled. "You're fighting sleep. I can see it in your eyes. Go ahead and relax, woman. Besides, I've got some reading to do."

She yawned again. "I just can't keep my eyes open any longer."

"I didn't realize my conversation was so boring," he teased.

"It's not boring." She hesitated. "It's soothing, like a tranquilizer. Thanks for listening."

"Anytime. Sweet dreams," he urged, pulling the blanket up over her left shoulder. "I'll defend you if anyone dares to say something about your snoring," he joked some more.

"You do that." She smiled, letting her eyes close.

Yvonne drifted into a deep slumber. Immediately she found herself in the middle of a dream surrounded by picturesque, crystal blue waters, sand the color of new sawdust, and sweltering temperatures. She had been walking on the beach with a man whose face she could not discern. They were strolling along the beach, holding hands, laughing and singing old love songs. He had laid out a colorful, handmade quilt for them and then dropped the picnic basket onto the blanket. His large, strong hands were soft and sensuous as he gently fed her chocolate-covered strawberries.

After eating a few dipped berries, she agreeably returned the action. The mysterious man had taken great delight in slowly nibbling at the strawberry until he had devoured it in its entirety. Then as if his hunger had yet to be assuaged, he began softly sucking the chocolate residue off her fingers. She moaned with great delight at the sensuous feeling, while the man continued to nibble his way up her arm, then her shoulder, then her neck, before finally resting his lips atop hers.

Without any warning, the dream shifted. Unexpectedly the kisses had ceased, and Yvonne's dream man had moved away from her, walking toward the ocean. Without saying a word, Yvonne watched him walk off into the sunset. The sun's reflection bounced off the water, making her vision blurred. A few seconds later, she found herself lying on the blanket with her eyes closed and the end of the day's sunshine peering down onto her face. Even through clamped eyelids, she could still see the light.

Sounds of waves cresting and crashing made for a relaxing, calming environment. Seagulls were swooning and squalling about the beach. The salty aroma of ocean water enticed Yvonne, while she lay peacefully enjoying the atmosphere.

The sudden overcast of darkness, appearing to be a

cloud blocking the sun's rays, in addition to the abrupt silence of the seagulls, disturbed Yvonne. Slowly she cracked open her eyes until they were wide and fully open and face to face with a shotgun barrel staring down at her.

"No!" she yelled audibly, before violently jerking upward in her seat, just as the boom of the gun sounded.

"Yvonne, Yvonne," Sean called to her, shaking her lightly. "Wake up. You're dreaming," he reminded her, rubbing the side of her wet face.

By now the people seated in the rows immediately in front, in back, and next to her were raised out of their seats, gawking with both concern and confusion.

"She's okay," Sean insisted, looking at each passenger staring their way. "Just a bad dream. That's all. Right, Yvonne?"

Her heart was still pounding erratically and her breathing desperate. Sweat engulfed her outer extremities as well as every body cavity known to man. *What was that all about? Why was she dreaming about a strange man trying to kill her?* She glanced over at Sean, who had his hand wrapped around her tiny hand, looking like a worried parent.

"Are you all right?" he questioned again.

Embarrassment had replaced Yvonne's retarded heart rate. Taking a deep breath, then exhaling it slowly, she murmured, "Yes. Thank you, Sean. I had a terrible dream," she said, shaking her head back and forth in disbelief. "Some strange man was trying to kill me."

Sean let his thick eyebrows crease into a concerned frown. "Well, thank God it was only a dream," he said, rubbing her hand some more. "Can I get you something else to drink?"

"Yes, please. A cold glass of water would be good."

Sean unfastened his seat belt and stepped into the aisle. Yvonne took the free moment to look over toward the passengers seated across from her. A young Asian child, no more than five years old, passed a comforting smile her way. The grin seemed to send a *I know exactly what you're going through, lady,* message. Yvonne returned the smile, then turned toward the front of the plane. Looking up at the TV screen hanging from the top of the plane, she let her mind wander into the movie. *Free Willy II* was just about to end.

Sean returned with two bottles of mineral water and a cup of ice. He handed Yvonne the cup and one of the bottles, then sat down in his seat.

"Let me get that for you," he said, untwisting the bottle cap.

"Thanks." She smiled. Chivalry. Nice. Must have had good home training. She had never experienced someone being so genuinely attentive to her needs so soon. It had taken Desmond practically nine months and constant reprimand from her to finally get him to take notice of somebody else's emotions besides his own.

The cool, refreshing taste of mineral water quenched Yvonne's thirst instantly. "Ah." She sighed, then licked her bottom lip. "Much better."

"I'm glad to hear that. I was a little concerned," he said, patting her on the hand.

The red light, highlighting the seat belt picture above them, flashed on. The captain's voice came over the speaker system, announcing that they were beginning their descent into Los Angeles.

"The weather in the Los Angeles area is overcast with a slight chance of showers. The temperature is fifty-one degrees. The time in Los Angeles is one thirty P.M. Enjoy your trip, and thank you for flying us."

Yvonne let out a loud breath. Her knees were stiff and her lower back cramped from sitting in one spot for too long. She was glad that the trip was almost over—although a small part of her would have preferred to loiter in Sean's presence a little longer under other less cramped conditions.

"Yvonne, I really enjoyed the few hours we've shared together. I'd like to spend some more time with you. That's if you're okay with the idea. Can I call you at your cousin's?" Sean asked as the flight attendant reached for their empty water bottles and cups.

Yvonne hesitated for a second, her heartbeat in overdrive once again. Now that the flight was almost over, she no longer had the confines of the cabin to tuck away her mixed emotions. It was easier, less pressure for her the way it was, just two people hanging out for a disclosed amount of time, sharing some space. Now Sean was aiming to change that by asking for Adrianne's phone number.

Regardless of Sean's comforting conversation during the six-hour flight, Yvonne had to remember that she had no intentions of opening up to another man anytime soon. Sure she felt an initial attraction to Sean, but that was as far as she really wanted it to go. Figuring that chances were he probably would not call anyway, Yvonne searched through her purse until she found her phone book and located Adrianne's phone number and address. What did she have to lose? But then what if he turned out to be a strange maniac, like the one holding the shotgun in her dream?

She placed her phone book back in her purse. "How

about I get your phone number instead?" That would be a safer bet, she thought, smiling up at him.

"Sure," Sean said, rifling through his wallet. "Not taking any chances, huh?" He handed Yvonne a business card.

Yvonne read the card and immediately tensed up, recalling what the skycap had told her before she left Atlanta.

"This card says Sean Germaine, Producer. I thought you said you were an airplane mechanic or something like that?" She frowned. She felt the walls closing in around her again. Should have just left things well enough alone, she thought, staring at the card.

"I am," he stuttered. "But I do this on the side." Sean noticed that Yvonne's face had become less friendly and more cautious. "I know what you're probably thinking, but that doesn't apply to me. I really am a producer on the side. You'll see," he said, unfastening his seat belt before standing.

The plane had landed, and the passengers began to spill into the rows. Sean reached up and opened the overhead compartment and pulled down his bag.

"Is your bag up here?"

"Yes," she said, crouching forward due to the tight space above her head. "It's the plaid bag with the tan handles."

Sean stepped aside so that she could exit from the row and then handed her the bag.

"Thank you," she said, waiting for the people in front of her to get their belongings together. "Guess this is it, Sean Germaine." Yvonne smiled broadly. "Thanks again for listening."

"The pleasure was all mine," he said, lifting her hand and kissing it softly. "I'll talk to you soon."

The passengers ahead of them started filing out one at a time. Halfway up the ramp, Yvonne glanced back over her shoulder. Sean was no longer behind her. He must have let a few other passengers go ahead of him. *Oh well, probably better that I don't see him anymore,* Yvonne thought, exiting the plane.

Reaching the inside of the terminal, Yvonne began the frantic search for Adrianne. She couldn't remember if they had agreed to meet at the baggage area or at the gate. With LAX being such an enormous airport, Yvonne began to wonder if she'd ever be able to locate Adrianne. She would give Adrianne a few more minutes, then make her way down to the baggage area. Maybe Adrianne was waiting for her there, she thought, leaning up against a column.

Sean tipped up behind Yvonne, causing her to jump.

"Sean . . ." She paused for a moment to compose herself again. "You scared me."

"I apologize." He smiled widely. "It was too tempting to pass up. Your cousin isn't here yet?"

"Not yet. But it's just like Adrianne to make a grand entrance," Yvonne said, scanning the area again. "I think I told her we'd meet at the baggage area. I don't know." She shrugged.

"Well," Sean said, stuffing his hands in his pockets. "We'll wait here for a while, then we can check the baggage area. How's that?"

Yvonne let out a comforting breath. She was happy that Sean was willing to stay by her side until she connected with Adrianne.

"I appreciate you waiting with me, Sean."

"Not a problem. I want to make sure you're not stranded here in this big city with no one to look after you. I'm not in a rush."

Minutes later, they had reached the baggage claim area. Yvonne took the opportunity to become familiar with the rest of Sean's physique. Besides standing at about six-two, he would be considered a stocky brother, somewhere between two hundred fifteen and two hundred twenty pounds. It was hard to tell because his outfit snuggled him just right. He had on a long-sleeved button-down cotton shirt with a denim vest.

His baggy jeans fit him perfectly. She hated to see brothers wearing skintight, crotch-crushing jeans. But that wasn't the case with Sean. His denims did just enough to highlight his mighty round butt without making him look ridiculously uncomfortable. *He sure is a luscious-looking brother,* Yvonne acknowledged internally.

Fifteen minutes and thirty bags later, their bags had finally swiveled around on the turnstile, and still there was no sign of Adrianne.

"Maybe she's waiting outside," Sean suggested. "Do you know what kind of car she's driving?"

"No," Yvonne said, lifting one of her three bags.

"I've got it," Sean insisted, picking up her bags. "Let's go outside and see if we can locate her. If not, we'll call her. And if she still isn't here, I'll drive you out to her house myself. How's that?"

Yvonne was taken aback by Sean's friendliness and genuine concern for her well-being. She liked the way he listened attentively as she relived her painful experience with Desmond. She enjoyed how Sean allowed her to be free to express her deepest feelings, concerns, and fear about being alone and not ever finding true love again. Yvonne had been captivated by Sean's tenderness, his advice about not giving up on men, brothers in particular, his comforting caress, and his handsome smile.

They walked outside into the midday sun, which was screened by an orange cloud. Several yellow taxi cabs lined the immediate curb, while other cars were double-parked on the other side. People were bustling about, trying to find their party or local shuttle services.

Squinting, with her hand over her forehead like she was about to salute someone, Yvonne searched for Adrianne. Sean stood back waiting, watching, and hoping that in a way Adrianne would not show up. The day was still young, and he wanted to spend some more time with this beautiful yet delicate sister.

Frustrated, Yvonne decided to go inside and phone Adrianne. Then she heard the familiar, high-pitched voice scream her name.

"Yvonne," Adrianne yelled from a moving car with her head hanging partly outside the window. "Over here." She waved frantically before stopping alongside one of the cabs. Adrianne clicked on her hazards, popped out of the silver, convertible Saab and ran over to Yvonne.

"Yvonne," Adrianne sang with extended arms, embracing her cousin. She had on a pair of winter white stretch pants with an orange ribbed sweater and pair of tan riding boots. The bright colored sweater accentuated her nut brown complexion.

"How are you? Sorry I'm late. The traffic is awful here. Look at you, Yvonne. You look good! Turn around and let me see your butt," she said, spinning Yvonne around. "Yup." She grinned, signaling some sort of approval. "Brothers out here go berserk over butts and boobs." She snickered.

"What's the deal with your hair? Don't worry. My stylist will take care of you." She slung back a lock of hair. "How you been? How was the flight? Are you hungry? Where's your bags?" Adrianne jabbered nonstop, while walking ahead of Yvonne.

The questions were rolling out of Adrianne's mouth so fast, Yvonne didn't have a chance to collect her thoughts, much less have a chance to reply to any of her questions. All she could do was grin. Actually if Adrianne had given Yvonne a chance to slip a word in, Yvonne would definitely ask her about that bright blond weave she had dangling down her back. The girl was absolutely impossible. She had almost forgotten how spotty and fickle Adrianne could be. Seeing Sean emerge from the background, Adrianne stopped dead in her tracks.

"Damn," she whispered to Yvonne. "He's fine! Who is that? You know him?"

"This is Sean," Yvonne said, tugging him by the arm softly. "Sean, this is my cousin, Adrianne."

"Nice to meet you." Adrianne flirted with a healthier than necessary grin. She faced Yvonne again and said, "You didn't tell me you were bringing a hunk with you."

"Oh, no. I met Sean on the plane," Yvonne quickly corrected.

"Really?" Adrianne said, eyeing him more intensely now.

Yvonne knew right away that she had made a mistake by making Sean sound so casual. If all things remained the same, chances were Adrianne would be on Sean licketysplit if Yvonne didn't hurry up and express her own interest in him.

"Sean has offered to show me the sights here in L.A.," Yvonne clarified.

"Good for you," Adrianne mumbled under her breath as she walked toward the car. "Sean, could you be a dear and put her bags in the trunk for me?"

Sean already had the bags in his grasp before Adrianne made her request. Reaching the back of the trunk, Sean carefully angled the bags, ensuring that they all would fit. Yvonne had moved away from the trunk and had already reached the passenger side of the car. Her back was facing Sean and Adrianne.

"Thanks for looking after my cousin, Sean. Perhaps you can swing by the Red Rooster later on this evening. A group of my associates are giving a happy hour there. Hope you can make it." She winked before sliding a four-by-six color flyer, and her business card slyly attached to the back of it, into his shirt pocket.

Sean hurried to the front of the car, where Yvonne stood waiting for Adrianne to unlock the car doors. Adrianne hit the electric locks. Sean reached around Yvonne and held the door open for her.

"Thanks again, Sean. I really enjoyed our conversation," Yvonne said, placing one leg into the car. "And don't mind Adrianne. She's borderline narcissistic," she teased, sitting down in the seat.

Sean chuckled softly, then whispered, "If she gets to be too much, call me—okay?"

"I will," Yvonne said, leaning out the window. "Thanks for the shoulder to lean on."

"Anytime," he said, squatting down. "I hope to hear from you soon. Be safe." He kissed her hand again then stood up.

"I will. See you, Sean."

With that, Adrianne shifted the car into first gear and screeched out into the lane. She was gaining steady momentum, when a couple of pedestrians stepped off the curb and into the middle of the street. Adrianne slammed on the brakes. Yvonne gripped the dashboard.

"Got-dang, California pedestrians," Adrianne cursed

aloud. "Hurry up!" she yelled through the windshield at the creeping couple lagging across the street.

"First thing you'll learn here, Yvonne. These crazy-ass, save-the-whales-and-ants-before-the-homeless, people always have the right of way."

"That is pretty ridiculous," Yvonne replied. "You almost killed us, trying to avoid them. They saw us coming. Why didn't they wait?"

" 'Cause you're in California now, and if you want to stay here, that's the way things are. California pedestrians always, always have the right of way whether they're in a crosswalk or not. Like these idiots crossing before us now." Adrianne sped off again, after the last pedestrian—a skinny elderly lady with a mink coat draped around her shoulder—jaywalked.

"Soooo," Adrianne said, getting the car under control. "What's the deal with Sean with his fine self? What did he say he did again?"

Yvonne laughed and shook her head back and forth. Too much L.A. sunshine had apparently sizzled some of her cousin's brain cells. "I believe he said he was an airplane mechanic or something like that," Yvonne finally replied. "I wasn't really paying that much attention," she lied.

A beeping sound rang throughout the car. Adrianne plucked the black pager from her leather satchel, clicked the gray button a few times, recited the numbers under her breath, before placing the pager back in her bag. The entrance to the freeway was only a few more blocks ahead.

"Really? An airplane mechanic, huh? Well, I suppose we all have to do what we have to do to make our contributions in the world. Are you tired? I can take you home so you get a little nap in before we head over to the happy hour tonight. It's going to be hella live. I heard some of the Dodgers and the Lakers, along with some local actors, will be there."

Hella live? Definitely an L.A. slang term, Yvonne thought, gazing out the window.

Adrianne reached below and pulled the cellular phone from under her seat, swerving wildly as she sprang up again. She pulled the car back into her lane before pressing in some phone numbers. Yvonne pushed her feet farther into the carpet mat, bracing for the collision. Thank God, Adrianne had gotten back into her own lane.

"Do you have something to wear?" Adrianne asked Yvonne, while shaking the cellular phone a few times before punching in the phone numbers again. "I sure hope you've grown out of that grandma wardrobe you used to wear when we were back at North Carolina A&T."

Adrianne dialed the number a third time—the car swerved again as she squeezed aggressively between a moving truck and a small sports car. "Tsk!" she huffed, passing the phone to Yvonne. "Put this in my bag for me. Damn battery is dead. I can't believe I forgot my adapter," Adrianne said, searching the ashtray for the cable.

"That was my girl, Fawn. She goes out with the star player for the Dodgers. You know who that is, don't you?"

Yvonne shrugged. She didn't know about any Dodgers' players, but what she did know was that Adrianne needed to concentrate on the road instead of her pager, cellular phone, Fawn, and her all-star Dodgers player.

"Do you always drive like this?" Yvonne questioned.

"Like what? Like this?" Adrianne asked, punching the accelerator down to the floor and passing a slow-moving, late-eighties BMW. "Piece of crap," she cried aloud, eyeing the driver intensely before zooming by him.

"I kind of like that car," Yvonne said, looking back over her shoulder.

"Yeah, you would," Adrianne quickly snapped. "If you don't have something fly to wear, I know I've got something in my closet that will be appropriate. Girl, out here, you've always got to be ready. Last week, I bumped into Arsenio and the week before that, I ran into Will Smith. You just never know, Yvonne."

Adrianne gabbed on and on unconsciously, merging onto the freeway. "So . . ." She paused only long enough to gaze into the rearview mirror at herself. "What really happened with you and Desmond? You only shared half the information over the phone. I want the juice—the un-cut, raw, and live version."

Yvonne shifted in her seat. She was getting agitated already. Not so much at Adrianne's constant blabbering but at her unwillingness to let the subject of Desmond come up when she felt like bringing it up. She crossed her arms in front of her chest, and kept silent—hoping that Biggie Smalls' "One More Chance" song would distract Adrianne.

Adrianne noticed, from the corner of her eye, that Yvonne's body language exuded a kind of I-don't-want-to-talk-about-it gesture. Choosing not to revisit the subject until Yvonne was ready to talk, Adrianne joined in with the lyrics to the song. She'd give Yvonne a few days. But after that, she'd keep at her until she 'fessed up the information about Desmond.

"I've got a few errands to run before we go out this evening. Would you like for me to drop you off at my place first so you can relax for a while?"

"That might be a good idea." Yvonne yawned. "I'm

feeling a little grimy and sticky from the flight. It won't cause you to go out of your way, will it?"

"This city is so spread out that anywhere you go in the L.A. area is usually out of the way." Adrianne laughed. "We'll be at my house in thirty minutes."

Adrianne timed their arrival perfectly, pulling into the ritzy community nineteen minutes later. The street was lined with scattered palm trees, and her town house faced the large, partly green mountain. The sun's rays were beginning to cut through the thinning smog. Adrianne reached overhead and punched the small, electronic object clipped onto her sun visor. The two-door garage door opened slowly, and Adrianne coasted the silver Saab inside.

"Here we are," Adrianne said proudly, stepping out of the car and walking toward the house door. "I know you'll love L.A. There's so much to do here, so many people to meet and date. Come on," she said, urging Yvonne to hurry. "Don't worry about the bags now. We'll get them before I go out again."

Yvonne followed Adrianne through the garage door, which led into a narrow hallway outside of the L-shaped kitchen. Upon reaching the living room, Adrianne waltzed over to the beige leather sofa and flopped down.

"I'm pooped." She exhaled hard.

"Very nicely decorated, Adrianne," Yvonne said, walking over to the marble fireplace and picking up a picture from the mantelpiece to inspect it further. "Hey, this is that actor who played in 'New Jack City.' " Perusing the rest of the photos displayed on the mantel, Yvonne noticed that Adrianne had several pictures hosting many stars and athletes. "You know all these people?" she questioned with amazement.

"Most of them. But some of them I just met while out at the clubs or some function. You wait," Adrianne said, rising off the sofa. "Pretty soon, you'll have a collection like that, too. You want something to drink?"

"Sure," Yvonne replied, continuing to gawk at the photos. God, she thought. How in the world did Adrianne know all these people? Is she really friends with these folks? Or has she been swept away by the L.A. star-crazed current?

Yvonne glanced around the room, taking in more of the decorations. The carpet was a light cream-color. All the Scandinavian-style furniture in the living room and dining room area were blanched in color. The thirty-gallon fish tank sat in the corner, full of foggy water but no fish. Adrianne had plenty of knickknacks and paintings strategically scattered about but no plants. Maybe she won't mind me picking up a few plants and bringing some life to the place, Yvonne hoped.

"Here you go, Yvonne," Adrianne said, handing Yvonne a glass of white grape juice. "I better go. If I get too comfortable, I won't want to move. I'll be back in a couple of hours. Make yourself comfortable. Let's get your bags out of the trunk."

Yvonne entered the house through the garage door, with two bags draped on her shoulder and two more in her hand. Slowly she dragged the bags up the stairs and to the far end of the hallway per Adrianne's directions. The guestroom was hued with peach and pink and might be considered bare by normal definition of a guest room.

A queen-sized bed with a few colorful pillows, a dresser with an empty silver picture frame, and a glass night table with a lamp and a telephone were the only items tucked away in the medium-sized bedroom. The large window faced the street with mountain peaks in the distant background. Across the hallway, directly facing her room, was the guest bathroom, hosting a full tub and the same peach and pink color scheme as the guest bedroom.

Yvonne grabbed one of the cotton, pink-faced rags off the towel rack, doused it with warm water, and washed her face. The next thing she did, after stripping off her clothes, was place that hideous-looking, plastic shower bonnet on her head before stepping into a hot, steaming shower. Standing with her back facing the shower nozzle, she let the force of the water pelt against her back and shoulders as she rolled her neck round and round.

Sitting in one position for such a long time had made her shoulders stiff. It had been a week since her last onset of frequent muscle spasms—something she battled with only when surrounded by tense and stressful situations. What she needed, she thought, while foaming her body with the freesia shower gel, was someone with strong hands, like Sean, to massage away the knots in her neck and shoulders.

Sean. Yvonne sensually toyed with his name. What a debonair name for such a majestic brother. Her mind slipped into a quick fantasy of him standing behind her in the shower, massaging her shoulders. As quickly as the fantasy had blazed, it subsided just as briskly, and Yvonne let out a deep sigh. She'd have to be very careful not to let her emotions overtake the good sense she had left.

Ten minutes and a foggy mirror later, Yvonne swung open the bathroom door and scurried across the hallway into her room. The temperature in L.A. was considered far less desirable by Californians than people currently resid- ing on the East Coast. Fifty degrees, the pilot had said when they landed at LAX. *Feels more like thirty degrees to me.* Yvonne shuddered, slipping into a long, silk lounging shirt. Throwing back the peach, pink, and white striped comforter, Yvonne slid down into the bed. Remembering she had to phone Aunt Gigi to let her know of her arrival, she sat back up.

She picked up the peach telephone and punched in zero, the ten digits, and then her calling card number. Aunt Gigi darn well better be home after all these numbers.

After three hollow rings, Aunt Gigi answered the phone. "Hello," she sang in her sweet southern voice.

"It's me, Aunt Gigi," Yvonne acknowledged. "I made it."

"Good, baby. How was your trip? Was your cousin there to pick you up on time?"

"Not really. But guess what?" Yvonne said, excitedly, wrapping the phone cord around her index finger. "I was seated next to a nice-looking brother."

"What?" Aunt Gigi replied astoundingly. "Is he someone you'd like to date? Does he live out there? Tell me all about him."

Yvonne took a moment to fill Aunt Gigi in with the particulars, highlighting, once again, Sean's admirable characteristics. "I felt so comfortable speaking with him, it was almost scary," Yvonne said, raising her knees up.

"Well, that's good, honey. You can never have too many gentlemen friends in your life, that's for certain. How are you going to get around?"

"I'll probably rent a car after a few days."

"Sounds good." Aunt Gigi paused, thinking of what else she could cover. "When are you going to call the law firm Douglass referred you to?"

"Monday morning. I figure I'd might as well enjoy the rest of this week and roam the city before delving into the workforce. I'd like to check out some of the local dance studios to see how soon I can get my youth program started." Yvonne yawned into the mouthpiece of the phone unintentionally. "I should go, Auntie. Adrianne has a full evening planned for us. So much so, she dropped me off so that I could get some rest."

"Some rest? What in God's name could be happening on a Wednesday night? You watch yourself out there with those people, Yvonne. Especially with that cousin of yours. She sounds like she's something else, if you ask me," Aunt Gigi warned.

"Who? Adrianne?" Yvonne chuckled. "She's all right, Aunt G. Quit worrying so much, okay?"

"Um-hmm," Aunt Gigi responded unimpressed. "You gonna be okay with money?"

"Yes, I'll be okay." Although she was a little concerned that Desmond hadn't returned her phone call regarding the sixty-five hundred dollars he owed her for the boat. "Don't worry."

"Okay, then. You take care of yourself and watch your back. I love you, baby."

"I love you, too, Aunt Gigi," Yvonne uttered before hanging up the phone and sliding under the covers. She rolled over onto her side and propped the two pillows under her head. Before drifting off into a slumber, Yvonne thought about the way Adrianne had leaped onto Sean at the airport. Maybe Aunt Gigi had a point. Naw, she dismissed quickly. They were both over that college incident with Robert Cole by now. Weren't they?

Four

Yvonne unfastened her seat belt, opened the passenger-side door, and cautiously slung her legs outside the car. Man, was she glad she chose the short black dress with its scoop neck and short sleeves over Adrianne's red, spandex and rayon blend, crotch-displaying miniskirt, she thought, standing up. She straightened out the dress, pulling it down and around her slender thighs. Aunt Gigi would have a coronary if she was here to witness Adrianne decked out in a skirt small enough for a twelve-year-old, a tiger print blouse tight enough for a six-year-old, and pantyhose-less legs arched in a pair of four-inch pumps.

She let out a disgruntled murmur. There wasn't anything wrong with the rayon and cotton cat-suit with the cinched waist that she was going to wear initially. But then Adrianne had convinced her that surely wearing such a conservative outfit would make her a mockery in L.A. That would be hard to live down. Yvonne sped up, trying to keep pace with Adrianne's strides.

"Explain to me again why we couldn't just meet your girlfriend at the happy hour."

Adrianne bent down to pick up her car keys she had dropped, exposing a little more buttock cheek than she probably meant.

"Because she's going to drive," Adrianne told her,

standing up straight again and tugging at her miniskirt. Slinging her hair to the side in a dramatic movement, she pressed the doorbell.

"Why does she need to drive?"

"She's going to drive because she has the new Benz," Adrianne replied.

"And we drove all the way out here because of that?" Yvonne asked a little miffed. That just doesn't make any sense, she thought, yawning. Fatigue was beginning to overwhelm her. It was already 9:20 P.M. by East Coast time, and if they didn't get to where they were supposed to be fairly soon, she would be ready to go to sleep in an hour.

"Yes, Yvonne. We drove out of our way so that we can glide to the happy hour in style."

"And the Saab wasn't stylish enough?" Yvonne asked.

"It'll do. But tonight we want to be recognized. We want to pull up next to Magic and the rest of the stars looking like stars, too." Adrianne rang the bell a second time, fluffing her hair while she waited.

"Is that a weave, Adrianne?" Yvonne asked. She had been working up enough nerve, since she landed in L.A., to ask Adrianne about all that *extra* hair. Yvonne had tried to let it lie, thinking maybe that regardless of the fact that Adrianne was her cousin, asking such a personal question might be inappropriate. But then all that slinging hair back and forth was too noticeable to ignore any longer. She averted her eyes toward the black iron gate encasing the mahogany door, while she waited for Adrianne to answer her question.

"What do you mean?" Adrianne said. She flung the honey blond-colored hair back in an exaggerated manner, then laughed.

Yvonne shook her head disapprovingly and laughed,

too. Lordy, Lordy, she looked so crazy with all that wild, bushy hair. If she even attempted to step foot back in their old New Jersey neighborhood, everybody would have a field day with her.

The front door swung open ferociously, displaying a short, short sister with an even shorter black dress on. She had eyebrow-raising reddish hair down to the middle of her back, long orange-painted fingernails, green-tinted eyes—obvious contact lenses—and way too much perfume, Yvonne thought.

"Heyyy," Fawn sang in an airy voice. "Let's go," she said hurriedly, locking the iron gate behind her before stepping down the two cement steps in her fishnet stockings and mega-inch sling-back pumps.

"Fawn, this is my cousin, Yvonne," Adrianne said, trailing behind her through the small patch of grass edged between the redwood-picket fence.

"Girl, what is up with them twist things in your hair?" she laughed, looking Yvonne over from head to toe. "So this the one with the fiancé and ex-girlfriend thing?" Fawn said, disengaging the alarm to the charcoal-colored luxury four-door sedan.

Yvonne's face grew warm with agitation. How did Fawn know about Desmond? Well, she knew the answer to that question but—still. She'd have to talk to Adrianne later about spreading her business with strangers.

"She is here in L.A., trying to make a brand new start." Adrianne headed for the front seat of the car.

"Not dressed all conservative like that," Fawn said, opening the car door. "Even got plain stockings on, too. Umph." Fawn cranked the ignition. "You plan on practicing law here?"

"I'm not sure," Yvonne said derisively, sitting down on the dark gray leather backseat.

The sounds of Snoop Doggy Dog and Dr. Dre burst through the speakers. "There's too many lawyers, if you ask me," Fawn volunteered, steering the car down the driveway toward the suburban city street. "I would never encourage our young kids to go to law school. It's a waste of time and money. I read somewhere that if we sent some of our lawyers to Japan, and they sent some of their engineers to the States, the world would be more intellectually proportioned."

"I heard that," Adrianne sang in unison. "Yvonne," she said, turning toward the back of the car to face her. "Did I tell you that Fawn just landed the lead role for a new sitcom, airing this fall."

"Really?" Yvonne said, a noninterested tone in her voice. "Did you get a lawyer to look over your contract?" There. That ought to quiet Ms. I-would-never-encourage-our-young-kids-to-go-to-law-school.

"Why waste the money? It wasn't that difficult. I did it myself," Fawn said, merging onto the freeway. "No offense, Yvonne, but lawyers are way overrated and way overpriced." She reached over and turned up the volume to the music. "Even the ones who never pass the bar."

Things still hadn't gotten off to a smooth sail with Fawn and Yvonne. Fawn was one of those sisters who thought everyone else was beneath her. Yvonne sighed. She didn't care for Fawn from the time she opened her front door. And then all that unwarranted derogatory verbiage about lawyers and the blatant way Fawn ignored her while she carried on a conversation with Adrianne, purposely leaving her out of the conversation. Rude. That's all it was. Whether she knew only two people in L.A. or not, Fawn would never be the third person she would spend any time with.

The club, a claustrophobic cubbyhole on the marina, was cramped with more scantily dressed Adriannes and Fawns. Yvonne furrowed her brow. She thought California was one of those states where smoking in clubs or in public was prohibited. She fanned her hand through the fog of smoke as she followed Adrianne and Fawn into the club and deeper into the sounds of Mariah Carey squealing through the speakers.

They careened around the crowded dance floor, toward the back of the club, where they waved down a brother hemmed up in a corner booth by two other brothers.

"Mikal," Adrianne yelled aloud. "Come on," she told Yvonne, yanking her by the hand and pulling her toward the booth. Fawn had veered off into the crowd, indulging some familiar-looking, soap opera-appearing brother with small chitchat.

"Mikal," Adrianne said dreamily. "I want you to meet my cousin, Yvonne." She turned to look at Yvonne. "Yvonne, this is *my friend,* Mikal. He's the man to know here in L.A.," she further added. "Isn't that right, Mikal?"

Mikal stood, eyes slowly perusing the lower half of Yvonne's body as he reached for her hand and as his eyes finally came into focus with her eyes. He lifted her hand to his lips and kissed it gently before speaking.

"Nice to make your acquaintance. Please," he said, pointing toward the empty part of the booth across from him. "Have a seat." Mikal's eyes followed Yvonne as she slid into the tight space first, followed by Adrianne.

"Did you all just get here?"

"Yes," Adrianne offered. "We would have been here sooner but, well, with Yvonne just getting into town, we—"

"Where did you come in from?" Mikal asked Yvonne, cutting off Adrianne's sentence.

"Atlanta," Yvonne replied. She eyed him speculatively. Lord have mercy. He was definitely one fine-looking brother. With all that babylike curly hair, dimples, and cool green eyes. Not to mention the gold expensive watch fastened to his wrist and the big championship ring of some sort gleaning vividly on his finger.

"Atlanta?" He smiled widely. "I know that city real well. Spent lots of years back and forth through there. What part?"

"Marietta. Off Cobb Highway."

"Really? I used to own a home over there. Not far from Life College." He lifted his drink and took a sip. "What brought you out here?"

"A long story," Yvonne replied tartly. She didn't mean to sound so bitchy, but then again she was still bitter about what had happened with Desmond, and she supposed there would be no hiding it.

"What you drinking, Mikal?" Adrianne said, attempting to change the subject. No need for Mikal to be so engrossed in her cousin's business.

"Pardon my manners," Mikal said, watching Adrianne. "What are you ladies drinking?" He waved for the waitress to come over to their booth.

"White zin, for me," Adrianne quickly offered, pulling back a lock of hair behind her ear.

"I'll have a Pepsi," Yvonne said, through a stifled yawn.

"Pepsi?" Adrianne taunted, while Mikal placed their orders with the waitress. "She'll have a red wine. If I re-member correctly."

"Adrianne," Yvonne whispered. "I don't want any wine right now."

Adrianne shook her head. "Okay, grandma. I'm begin-ning to wonder why you and Desmond didn't work things out," she said through clutched lips.

Yvonne shot her a wicked glare. "Don't go there, Adri-anne. It's not necessary. I'm already tired, and a glass of wine is not what I need unless you want to see my head crashed down on this table." She let out another yawn through splayed fingers across her mouth.

Mikal looked down at his watch. "It's only ten twenty-three for you. Don't tell me you're tired already?" Mikal asked in a stirring tone, piercing her gaze with his eyes.

"A little," Yvonne confessed. "It's been a long day." She smiled faintly, unsure of how to play Mikal. If she wasn't mistaken, she thought that Adrianne may have a hidden fondness toward him. She'd have to tread lightly—careful not to let another Robert Cole incident take place between them.

Mikal was handsome and charming and obviously free with his money, she thought, as she watched him give the waitress a ten dollar bill and sent her away when she tried to give him his change. Surely a glass of wine and a glass of Pepsi didn't tally to ten dollars. Did it?

"Your day may have to be just a little longer." Mikal grinned seductively over Toni Braxton's love ballad. God, she was a strikingly attractive-looking woman—dark-complected, classy, and elegant—just like he liked them. Unlike *some* of the trashy women he had been dealing with over the past few years.

Yvonne just might be the kind of woman he had been

searching for. A southern-style woman with morals, backbone, and ethics. And a new woman in town, untainted with the deceit and lies and sticky fingers that L.A. harbored. A fairly naive woman who didn't know as much about the L.A. streets and L.A. ways like he did. He'd have to get with Adrianne later on the side and get the four-one-one on Ms. Marietta, GA.

Yvonne stared into her glass, taking a few sips of the Pepsi, hoping that when she looked up again she wouldn't come face to face with Mikal's olive-shaded eyes. Um, well, there was a wish wasted, she thought, lifting her gaze from the syrupy beverage only to be welcomed with Mikal's. His intense stare made her nervous. Was this how it was now between men and women when they first met, she wondered, sucking on the straw.

"I spoke to my friend in D.C. about that tax question you had," Adrianne said, trying to break the gaze between Mikal and Yvonne. "He's going to look into it and get back to me so I can proceed with your packet."

"That's good," Mikal replied, still not looking at Adrianne. "Let me know when you find out." He paused for a minute, then continued. "Yvonne," he said, leaning closer into the table. "Would you like to dance?"

Just then a tall brother approached the table and greeted them. "Good evening everyone," Sean said.

"Sean?" Yvonne nearly shrieked.

Good evening, everyone? Where the hell is this Negro from talking like that? Mikal wondered quietly.

Thank God. Adrianne beamed inwardly. Now Mikal can get out of Yvonne's face for a few minutes.

"What are you doing here?" Yvonne asked.

Sean pulled the flyer out of his pants pocket and waved it back and forth a few times. "Compliments of Adrianne."

He smiled. "Sean," he said, extending his hand toward Mikal.

Mikal, still seated, took his hand and responded, "Mikal. Here," he said, standing. "Take my seat. Me and Yvonne was just about to head out to the dance floor. Ready, Yvonne?"

Adrianne stood up to allow Yvonne room to slide back out of the cramped space. But then she turned to Mikal and said, "Let's you and I dance instead. Give Sean and Yvonne here a chance to get more familiar."

Yvonne stopped sliding across the bench seat, Sean sat down in Mikal's spot, and Mikal reluctantly lead Adrianne out to the dance floor.

"I'm not going to stay long," Sean told her. "Just thought I'd stop by hoping you'd be here to indulge me in a dance or some dinner."

"Dinner?" Yvonne smiled.

"Yes, dinner. If you haven't eaten already."

"I had the California yogurt with the nut topping thing before we left the house. But nothing serious since that scrumptious meal on the plane a few hours ago." She laughed.

"There's a little Caribbean restaurant called the Caribe, next door, we can check out," Sean said, with raised brows. "Would you care to skip over there and grab a bite to eat with me?"

"Sure," Yvonne said promptly. "All this smoke is driving me crazy." *Along with the weird vibe she was getting from Mikal,* she thought, scooting to the edge of the burgundy vinyl booth seat. She stood up with Sean, brushing the lap of her dress. "Let me go tell Adrianne where we're going. I'll be back."

She left Sean standing there at the booth, eyeing her

buttocks, she was sure. Adrianne and Mikal were close to the edge of the dance floor, making it easy for her to whisper into Adrianne's ear her plans to go to the restaurant next door with Sean.

"Don't leave without me. We should be back in an hour or so, okay?"

Adrianne smiled at Yvonne and nodded in the affirmative, before happily continuing her dance with Mikal.

Mikal followed the sway of Yvonne's hips back to the table, where she took off toward the back door exit with Sean. A look of displeasure blanketed his face. Where the hell did she think she was going? She still owed him a dance. A jazz ballad by Nancy Wilson replaced the dancing beat of Brandy. Mikal exited the dance floor with Adrianne trailing behind him.

"Where did Yvonne go?"

"Why?" Adrianne responded gruffly.

" 'Cause I want to know. Who's that brother she's with?"

"A friend."

Mikal turned sharply to face her. "Adrianne, if you know like I know, you'd better keep an eye on your cousin if you don't want anything to happen to her in this cesspool city. You've been pretty fortunate so far. Driving a brand new Saab and living the high life outside of Orange County. Be careful," he said, with a half smirk. "Now if you need anyone to keep an eye on your cousin, I'm the man. Not some King's English-speaking brother."

Mikal flagged the waitress over before sitting down at the booth. He pointed toward the seat across from him, summoning Adrianne to sit down as well.

Adrianne's face was filled with hostility. She watched Mikal pour his charm on the waitress as she hustled away to fetch him another drink. Such the ladies' man, she thought resentfully. Yvonne had been in the city less than twenty-four hours, and already she was causing more trouble than she could even care to imagine. Damn her and her saintly demeanor, Adrianne thought, slumping back against the booth.

Adrianne took a sip of her wine, contemplating Mikal's obvious stake in Yvonne.

"She's been through a lot, Mikal. She ain't ready for—"

Mikal held up his hand, gesturing stop. "Save your breath, Adrianne. It's not going to work. You already know this. Just sit back and enjoy your drink. Life is too short. You never know when your number has been punched. Relax," he said. "There's a price to pay for everything. Remember that. Now where did Yvonne and Mr. Sean skip off to?"

Adrianne let out a deep sigh, cutting her eyes toward the back of her head before looking at Mikal. "I don't know," she finally lied. "She said he's going to bring her home later. That's all I know." She lifted her glass and took a swallow, smirking inwardly. *And that's all you need to know, too.*

Five

Yvonne walked past the makeshift stage, cramped with rattan stools and steel drums, as she made way to the table she shared with Sean. The Jamaican and Trinidadian flags hung in the backdrop. The band was taking a break and was scattering about the cozy, colorful, candlelit restaurant. A reggae song by Bunny Wailer crackled through the small speakers hanging from the ceiling.

"I was beginning to think you snuck out the back door," Sean teased, rising from his seat to allow Yvonne to sit down.

"Of course not. The ladies' room was packed." She grinned, feeling a little more sedate and relaxed than she had an hour ago. "Too much of that rum punch," she said, with a pat on her belly.

Sean laughed. "Tell me about it. And imagine, we only had the lightweight version."

"They have different versions?"

"They have to. Most people have to drive home after they leave here. You can drink the heavyweight version only if you have a designated driver."

"Oh, I see," Yvonne said, biting into another plantain and lightly rocking to the reggae beat.

"Glad to see you enjoyed the food," Sean said, looking down at the near empty plates of jerk chicken, plantain, curried shrimp, and roti they had ordered together. It was good to see a woman with a healthy appetite for a change, as opposed to the women he had dated who ate like little birds—always peeking and picking over their food.

Sean eyed her more thoroughly. She had certainly warmed up to him since he had bumped into her at the magazine rack in Atlanta's airport some twelve hours earlier. See what a little time can do? He bent a smile. Nobody knows time but time, but then time don't even know time sometimes. He had to be careful not to come on too strong, to run her underground with her fragile heart and hidden fears and mistrust of men.

He enjoyed their time. Even felt like he knew her all of his life. Then that's what he supposed the word *destiny* was all about. Things shouldn't be that difficult if you meet the right person, if you gel with the right individual—if you have the opportunity to sit across from an innocent-looking, beautiful sister named Yvonne.

"So," he said, after another sip of punch. "What are you doing tomorrow?"

Yvonne shrugged. "I need to set up an interview so I can be among the employed folks of L.A." She smirked.

"What's your specialty?"

"What's my specialty?" She pondered, repeating Sean's question. If she had to pick one, it would definitely be teaching dance. Though being a lawyer was what would put food in her belly, dancing was her first true passion. "I guess it would be law," she finally replied.

"Law? Really?" Sean said with a furrowed brow. "Then I take it you're a lawyer."

"I guess," Yvonne said sourly. She played with the umbrella stirrer that sat in her empty glass of lemonade.

"You don't sound too enthused," Sean said.

She leaned against the back of the bamboo chair. "To be honest with you, Sean, it's sad to say, but I don't even know if I really want to practice law."

"Why is that? Being a lawyer seems quite admirable."

"Not when there is something else you'd rather be doing," she told him.

"Well, what would you rather be doing?"

"Dancing."

"Dancing?"

"Yes, I'd rather be dancing. Teaching underprivileged kids to immerse themselves into dancing instead of things that could get them into trouble."

Sean leaned back into his chair. *Dancing?* "You're a dancer, too? Go-go dancer, erotic dancer, what?" He laughed.

Yvonne laughed, too. "If I want to be." She winked.

Um, Sean thought, letting his eyes helplessly wander over the top half of her body. Her breasts were smaller than he would have liked, but he still could imagine her dressed in a skimpy bikini top and bottom, dancing for him. He snapped his mind free from his lustful thoughts. How inappropriate, he reprimanded himself, sitting up straighter.

"But seriously," Yvonne finally said, "I taught African and modern dance to impoverished children throughout Atlanta."

"Impressive," Sean said. "If more brothers and sisters took the time to nurture and give back to our children, things wouldn't seem all so hopeless to them."

"Exactly," Yvonne agreed. "I know for me, it's the best reward I could ever ask for."

"I know—I've been trying to do the same thing with my production company."

"Is that right?"

"Every couple of months, I get a group of young children together, who are aspiring musicians, writers, directors, producers, actors, and actresses and we sit down and sketch out a musical skit to perform for a local church or organization. The proceeds are divided among the children."

"Wow," Yvonne replied in amazement. "That's what I'd call impressive."

Sean shrugged. "Yeah, well, we all have to do our part to help the community. Maybe we'll have a chance to collaborate on some projects later on. You could start by teaching me a few steps."

"We can start right now," Yvonne said, standing. The band had returned from its break and was tapping away on the steel drums.

Sean looked a bit uncomfortable at first at the thought of being on the dance floor with a professional dancer, so to speak. But seeing Yvonne's face and body swaying so happily with the music, he decided to relax and have fun. He stood up and took her hand, making a way through the small crowd toward the parquet dance floor.

Psychedelic ball-shaped lights rotated round and round, giving the dance floor a disco-tech feeling. The beat was fast, inviting the patrons on the dance floor to let it all hang loose.

Yvonne shimmied her shoulders back and forth, arching backward. She turned and snapped and popped her fingers and shuffled her feet. Sean did his best to keep up with the same dance steps as Yvonne but found that he was a lot stiffer than she would probably ever be.

The calypso-style band kept the pace of the music fast for the next several minutes, ensuring that its participating patrons got a full cardiovascular workout. After twenty-five minutes or so, the band turned the rhythm down to a slow, melodic beat. The singer of the band led a soulful ballad. Sean grabbed Yvonne by the waist and drew her into his chest.

Yvonne's heart skipped. Being drawn so close to Sean scared her. The sweet smell of his cologne, and the heat emanating from beneath the leather vest he had partially unzipped, exposing his hard chest, excited her.

Umph—she just wanted to bury her lips dead smack into the middle of his chest, tasting the tightly curled pieces of hair striating throughout. If she didn't watch herself, she could easily be snuggled up with him somewhere cozy without an L.A. or Georgia care in the world.

Sean rubbed the lower part of Yvonne's back. God, the side of Yvonne's baby-soft face planted dab center in the crevice of his chest was a feeling he hadn't experienced in some time. If Yvonne didn't stop brushing his chest hairs with the movements of her cheek, and quit showering his chest with her warm breath, she was going to feel something not so soft pressing against her lower thigh. He ran his fingers up the nape of her neck, massaging the lower part of her head.

Yvonne felt the same chill zip through her body that she had felt earlier when she and Sean touched each other on the plane. Sean's fingers rummaging through her hair was a definite weak spot for her. Hypnotically she arched her head upward, peering at the side of his face. The music, the atmosphere, the rum punch—something was sucking her in.

He didn't want to smother her lips with his—didn't mean to come to a complete standstill on the dance floor, sucking lips with a woman like during his high school days. But he couldn't help himself—didn't even want to help himself. The kiss lingered on and on like the trailing end of an old Isley Brothers' love ballad.

Yvonne wanted to break free—knew it wasn't right to be standing in the middle of a restaurant dance floor, kissing a man she had barely met. But she was in Los Angeles, California, now and not a worry in the world that any one of the other five couples bopping on the dance floor knew who she was. This revelation allowed her to let Sean have free rein of her tongue—allowed him to swirl her tongue around so much, so softly, that she was dizzy by the time the song ended and the person standing behind her tapped her shoulder a second time.

The band had already picked up the beat by the time Yvonne turned to face the person who had touched her shoulder. Adrianne stood on the dance floor, next to Mikal, with an astonished look on her face.

Adrianne cleared her throat. "Enjoying ourselves, are we?" she said, sneaking up behind Yvonne. "I just came by to tell you that we were about to leave."

"I can take you home later if you'd like, Yvonne," Sean happily offered. "Where do you live, Adrianne?"

"Outside of Orange County. Yvonne knows the address. Don't you, Yvonne?"

Yvonne nodded yes, all the while studying Sean's face. Oddly she no longer felt reserved about him. "If it's not out of your way," she finally said.

"Not at all." He smiled, grabbing her hand, and initiating the dancing again.

"Here's the house key," Adrianne said, pulling off the house key from her ring of keys and handing it to her.

"How are you going to get in?" Yvonne questioned.

"I'll get in. Have a good time." She winked.

Adrianne turned to face Mikal, who was looking dejected and lost. Adrianne shrugged her shoulders and stepped away from the dance floor. "He's taking her home," she said, walking toward the exit doors.

Mikal stood staring at Yvonne, who was gazing at Sean, who was eyeing him. Yeah, he had her for now—had even gotten a leg up on him by kissing her first. But that was a fluke. There was no way Sean was going to have her straddling atop of him before he had a chance to make her his.

Mikal stepped outside into the balmy marina air, where two thick-necked brothers waited patiently for his return. They proceeded toward the Red Rooster parking lot, where Adrianne was talking with Fawn and two other men. He purposely beelined toward the back of some bushes to avoid Adrianne and the blabbermouth Fawn. He had a bigger picture in mind other than rumbling between the sheets with Adrianne and the rest of her cronies. He was going to make Yvonne his new prize girl if it took somebody else's last breath away.

Six

Adrianne popped two Advils in her mouth, chasing them down with a glass of tap water. Her head was throbbing from an overdose of wine from the night before. She poured a second cup of the tart coffee, glancing at the coffeemaker's clock, which read 7:20 A.M. She took her seat at the tiny wooden table, took a few cautious sips of coffee, and resumed reading the business section of the newspaper.

Hearing Yvonne making her way toward the kitchen, Adrianne looked up from her paper, turning to face her. "You're up early," she said, eyeing her attire.

It was late March, and Yvonne was dressed in a pair of khaki pants, sneakers, and a Polo pullover shirt. Now where the hell was she going, looking all matronly like this this morning? Adrianne wanted to scream.

"I have a nine o'clock tee-off with Sean." Yvonne beamed.

"Tee-off? What you know about golf?" Adrianne laughed.

"Not a darn thing." Yvonne joined in with the laughter. "But Sean has offered to teach me."

"Girl, it's forty-nine degrees outside. How are you'll going to play golf in all that dew outside?"

Yvonne shrugged. "I don't know. Just sounds like fun."

"Fun or not, you'd better take a sweater with you to keep warm. At least until it warms up."

"Well, how hot does it get in the daytime this time of year?"

"Low sixties. Depends. We've been having a weird season. This is supposed to be the rainy season," Adrianne said, rising from the table, wrapping her terry bathrobe shut again. "You want some raisin bread or some coffee? Or I have some bran cereal and yogurt."

"Don't you have something a little more, um, less California-like? Like some grits and eggs or pancakes and sausage?"

"Girl, I don't mess around with that artery-clogging crap no more. Ya need to think about giving up all that clumpy cholesterol stuff." She dumped the remainder of the coffee into the sink, rinsed out the cup, and turned it upside down in the drain. "What time did sexy Sean drop you off?"

"About twelve forty-five. Somewhere around there." Yvonne smiled brightly, but her head was buried too far into the refrigerator for Adrianne to see her glowing.

"Seems like you were having a good time—for someone who just got into the city," Adrianne said with a raised eyebrow. "You plan on spending a lot of time with him?"

"Hard to tell yet. We'll see," Yvonne told her, while pouring a glass of orange juice.

"I think Sean will be good for you. Keep your mind off of Desmond." *And keep you from Mikal's eyesight, too.* "Oh, before I forget, I need to get that key from you." She reached into the kitchen drawer nearest the stove. "Here's a spare key to the house. And you have my pager and cellular numbers, right?"

"Right," Yvonne said, taking the key chain, with the

little brass Coach purse dangling from the end of it, from Adrianne. She tucked it into her pocketbook and handed the other key to Adrianne.

"All right, girl." Adrianne smiled and took the key from her. "Tax time is right around the corner. I need to finish some paperwork for a client. Leave a message if you decide not to come home. This is a big scandalous city—so heads up," she said, leaving the kitchen area. "If you need some condoms, I've got a box under the sink in my bathroom," she called out. "Help yourself."

Yvonne stood in front of the mantelpiece, eyeing the many photographs of famous people again. Sean was due to arrive in a few minutes, and she was feeling a bit nervous. She just couldn't believe that Adrianne knew all these people. She drew the picture of the three men standing in black tuxedos closer to inspect. She recognized the man in the middle of the trio, easily. It was Mikal, surrounded by another man she was sure she had seen in some movie or on some talk show. The other brother didn't ring a bell, like the bell that was chiming through the house right now.

Looking out the peephole, Yvonne felt her cheeks grow warm with excitement upon seeing Sean standing on the opposite side of the door. She counted to three, then unlocked the door.

"Good morning," she said, swinging open the heavy door.

"Good morning," Sean said, pulling a long, exotic flower from behind his back. "For you."

"How sweet," Yvonne said, sniffing the orange and blue flower. "Thank you. It's beautiful."

"A true reflection of the person holding it." Sean bent down and placed a kiss on her lips.

Yvonne responded easily. Lord help her. She didn't want to get sucked in by this mere stranger. She pulled away from the magnetism, backing into the foyer.

"You want a glass of orange juice or coffee?"

"No, thank you," Sean said, stepping into the foyer behind her. "I thought we'd get a bite to eat at the lodge before we teed-off. You ready?"

"Ready," she said, grabbing her purse. "Should I grab a sweater or something first?"

"No need. I've got an extra jacket just for you." He smiled.

"Just for me, huh?" she said, locking the door behind her.

"Just for you," Sean said, pulling her into his embrace before locking lips with her a second time.

Just what was he doing? Sean wondered, opening the car door for Yvonne. The last time he had responded so strongly to a woman was back in 1982 when he was a sophomore at the University of Pittsburgh. Natalie Goodens had wrapped him in a whirlwind the same way Yvonne was threatening to do. They had been a steady item for five years. Until that dreadful night—the night that had changed his life forever.

They pulled into the parking lot of the nine-hole golf course, which most beginners frequented in order to get a grip on their game. The morning mist didn't provide for an ideal day on the course, but that would all change come two hours or so.

He shut off the engine, glanced over at Yvonne, and said, "Ready?"

"Ready," she said, stepping out of the car.

"We'll hit a few balls first so you can get a feel for it, and then we'll head over to the greens." He grabbed the golf bag, slung it over his shoulder, and headed for the driving range. His cleated golf shoes, with the two-tone tan and brown flap, clicked across the concrete like a tap dancer skirting across the stage.

Propping his golf bag against the fence, he motioned for Yvonne to wait and watch a few of the other people swing, while he went to retrieve a bucket of colorful golf balls. He tap danced back past Yvonne toward the front desk.

"Okay," he said, lifting a number three club from the green nylon and cotton bag with leather straps. He guided her to the area, gave her the iron, and stood behind her.

"Plant your legs," he coached. "And bend your knees. Yes, like that," he said, pulling her elbows in and pushing her hips down. "Relax and take a couple of practice swings."

He backed away from her, giving her room to swing. All that close-up activity reminded him that it had been too long since he had felt the soft cushion of a woman's backside pressed into his lap. If he wanted to concentrate on teaching Yvonne the game, he'd have to keep some distance between them.

"Like this?" Yvonne asked, swinging awkwardly.

Sean smiled. "Something like that. Relax your arms a little." He watched her try her swing again. Not bad, he thought, grinning. The fact that she was even willing to indulge him in a game of golf was impressive enough.

"Always keep your head down and your eye on the ball. Okay?"

"Okay," she said, keeping her eye focused on the ball.

"You ready?"

"Hope I don't embarrass you too much." She chuckled nervously.

"You won't. Just keep playing with the club until it feels comfortable to you," Sean said, dumping several golf balls into the flat, octagon-shaped steel pan. "You probably won't hit it past the fifty-yard line at first. So don't bother to hit it hard. Just get used to hitting it, and then we'll get you up to par. No pun intended." He smiled.

He placed the first golf ball, a yellow one with red writing advertising some high-tech company, on the rubber tube-like tee in the range next to her. "Do your thing, babyyyy," Sean teased Yvonne, grabbing a number eight. "I'll be right here if you need me."

Yvonne scattered her feet wider then closer then wider; she straightened her elbow, then loosened it then stiffened it again; she squatted lower then stood up higher then squatted lower again. Finally she took a wild, powerful swing at the ball. Nothing but air. She missed the entire ball. She laughed.

Sean gave her an encouraging nod of the head. "It takes a while, but once you get comfortable with your stance, it'll get better." He loaded a ball onto the tee, took a few practice swings, and slammed the iron against the yellow ball. The shot marked somewhere between the fifty- and one-hundred-yard area. He grimaced.

Yvonne watched Sean as he set up for another swing. His form and follow-through were much better than she could ever hope to have. Copying Sean's actions, she bent forward, selected another ball, and loaded it onto the tee.

She never could understand what all the fuss was about this little ball. But then as she tried unsuccessfully, for a second time, to hit the hard, tiny ball, she realized it was more challenging than she had ever imagined.

Sean had captured his swinging groove by now, slamming home three balls in a row past the two-hundred-yard mark. Being chilly in Atlanta for more than two weeks, and cooped up in a toasty house, was punishment in the worst form. Reaching into the bag, he replaced the number eight iron and withdrew the number six.

He took a moment to watch Yvonne, checking to make sure she was indeed grasping the concept of things. Her form was gluing together, though it left a lot to be desired. Perhaps if she enjoyed the game enough, he would consider enrolling her in a few private lessons with Dan, his private instructor. She lowered her arm, took a big swing, finally connecting for a mark a little past the fifty-yard area.

"See, you got it already." Sean smiled, stepping back onto his platform.

"It still feels dorky. My hips are all twisted to the side, and my knees are puckered out, and my behind is all propped up." She laughed, taking another swing. "But I'm sure all beginners go through the same thing."

"Exactly," Sean told her, unintentionally hitting his ball toward the left of the field.

"Who picks up all those balls out there?" Yvonne pulled back on her swing, midway into her stroke, causing her last ball to veer right.

"The first-timers." Sean grinned. "I didn't tell you that?"

"Yeah, right." She smirked. "We might as well pack it up now then."

Sean grabbed the iron from her and placed it into the bag, handing her another iron. "Try this one for a while now."

"But I'm out of balls," she said, taking the iron.

"Here," he said, lifting up his tray and dumping a few golf balls into her pan. "I've got plenty of balls." Sean grinned seductively.

Yeah, I'm sure you do, Yvonne wanted to say aloud but resisted the temptation.

Sean stood back observing Yvonne's follow-through once more. Okay, so she wasn't the best stroke he had seen out here since he picked up the game three years ago. But she was most certainly the finest. He watched her inadvertently chuck the last ball well short of the fifty-yard mark. She turned to face him, shoulders hunched upward as she did.

"Let's do it," Sean said, signaling her to walk ahead before he lifted the bag.

"There's a few things you should know," he told her, standing the bag upright, a few feet from the first hole. "If you hear someone yell *fore,* it means a ball might be coming your way, so duck."

Pulling out the pitching wedge iron, he continued. "See where those guys are, over there?" He pointed to a plush patch of green some hundred yards across a narrow stream. Yvonne nodded. "Notice the flagpole the guy is holding? We have to wait until those players place the flag pole back in the hole and leave the green before we take our turn. Okay?"

Yvonne squinted hard. "You mean I'm suppose to hit the ball all the way over there?"

"Yup," Sean agreed, pulling out a handful of wooden tees from the zipper portion of his bag.

"How many chances do I get?" she asked, turning serious.

"This is a par three course. That means you're suppose to make it in the hole in three strokes or chances." He handed her a couple of tees.

"Ssss," Yvonne hissed, glancing down at her open palm. Three tries? Hardly probable. "What are these?"

"This is how you hit the ball. A tee at each hole. They're called tees. I hear some brother invented them, but I forgot his name. Anyway, this is how you hold it." He wedged the tee between his pointer and middle finger, grabbed the ball, and laid it atop the flat-head portion of the wooden tee and planted it into the ground. "See? You try it."

Yvonne clasped the blond-colored piece of wood between her two fingers, just like Sean had done with his. She placed the ball in her hand and attempted to stick the tee, with the ball on top, like Sean had done—to no avail though, because the ball rolled off and onto the damp grass. She picked up the ball and placed it atop the tee.

"Here you go," Sean said, handing her an iron. "Just relax, take a couple of practice swings, and let it rip."

She took the driver iron, stood off to the left of the ball, and began getting her posture together. "But what if I hit it into the stream?"

"We've got a pitching wedge, a sand wedge, but no water wedge." He laughed. "Trust me, Yvonne. You won't hit the ball in the stream because you won't want to get down there to hit it out." He was teasing about the getting in the water part, but she didn't have to know that. All she needed to do was hit the ball.

Yvonne stood stiffly at first, trying to feel for her stroke. She looked up at the green, then back down at the ball. Then up at the green and back down at the ball again.

"Make sure you keep your head down and your eye on the ball," Sean encouraged. "Now give a little sexy wiggle, let the boys know you're out here, and put all you got into it. The club will do the rest."

He stood back and examined Yvonne's modestly plump butt. *Nice. Very, very nice.* When his eyes finally came up, she had slammed the ball well past the stream of water and onto the green about seven feet away from the hole. *Ain't this about a . . . Just like a beginner to get off a lucky shot like that.*

He stepped forward to tee-off. "You sure you haven't played this game before?"

"I'm sure." Yvonne smiled.

Sean took a few practice swings before hitting the ball across the stream and onto the green, next to Yvonne's ball. "After you, my dear," he said, lifting the bag again and trailing behind Yvonne.

God, he'd have to be careful not to get yanked in again, or pull Yvonne in. He wasn't prepared to do that deep love thing again. No matter how much he enjoyed their time together. No matter how beautiful and drawn he was to Yvonne, he would never fall all the way in if he could help it. He had made that promise to himself and had all intentions of trying to hold fast to it.

Seven

Yvonne had heard about the love at first sight occurrence. Even had a few acquaintances who claimed their current spouses were an example of said phenomenon. But to experience it on her own was a totally different perspective. She laced the tops of her sneakers before stepping out of the room.

She could hear Adrianne talking in the background. Yvonne crossed the hallway to Adrianne's room, which was adjacent to her room. The high-pitched sound level of Adrianne's voice let her know that she was upset with the person she was speaking with.

"I told you, I don't know, Mikal," Adrianne was saying. "We'll play it by ear. I don't understand what the big deal is. She's got plans."

Yvonne stood beneath the archway of Adrianne's bedroom door. *Who is she talking to? Mikal?* Yvonne scanned Adrianne's bedroom, taking special notice of the king-sized bed with the wrought-iron headboard and footboard. Such a big bed for a small person. She noted the matching night stands that sat on each side of the bed. One with a vase filled with fresh-cut flowers and the other, near where Adrianne sat, with the sleek, modish telephone with the built-in clock alarm and answering machine.

"I said I'll try! Now relax. Well, if you weren't so preoccupied—" Adrianne stopped talking, turned, and acknowledged Yvonne standing in the doorway. She covered the mouthpiece of the phone and said to Yvonne, "I'll be right down. Go ahead and grab some juice or something."

"Okay," Yvonne said, before turning to make her way down the hallway toward the steep steps.

It was 11:00 A.M., and she and Adrianne were supposed to meet Fawn and one of her other friends, Kala, for brunch and shopping. That was fine, Yvonne thought, thumbing through yesterday's newspaper as she sat down at the table. She didn't particularly care for Fawn, but she was always interested in shopping. Even if she didn't have any extra money to splurge.

There was no way she'd even think about putting one single additional thing on her American Express card until it was paid off. Until Desmond coughed up the sixty-five hundred dollars he rightfully owed her. She had tried to reach him again earlier this morning, but his assistant confirmed that he was out of town until next week. Figures.

Yvonne sighed. She had worked so hard to keep her credit together. She had planned to use her strong credit as leverage to purchase a dance studio of her own in the near future. And Desmond Rappaport was not about to ruin that dream for her.

Unconsciously she flipped through the pages of the *Los Angeles Times,* until she found a caption that caught her interest. On the fifth page of the What's Happening in Your Area section of the newspaper, her eyes read: City of Davis to spend $100,000 to build an underground tunnel for frogs to cross the intersection.

Yvonne began to laugh, lightly at first, before falling out into a bout of hysteria. They have got to be kidding, she thought, rereading the caption again before engaging in the three-paragraph article. Build a tunnel for one hundred thousand dollars so the frogs can get across the street? How ludicrous. She chuckled some more.

Adrianne had come downstairs in the middle of Yvonne's paroxysm—standing in the walkway between the kitchen and dining area, gawking at her.

"Share the laughter," Adrianne said.

"This article," Yvonne said, still snickering. "They can't be serious." She looked up at Adrianne, who seemed somewhat annoyed. "The city of Davis wants to invest one hundred thousand dollars for a tunnel." Yvonne paused to let out another chortle. "For the frogs who keep getting splattered by cars traveling on the road." She wiped her eyes. The whole thing was too unrealistic to be true. Why, she'd never seen an article of such compassion for animals in all her life. She was definitely on the left side of the country.

"Yeah, I read that, too." Adrianne smiled partially. "You ready?"

Yvonne creased the paper back into its fold and stood up. "Ready. Do you think we'll be back by four o'clock?"

"Why?" Adrianne said, grabbing her purse and keys.

"Because I'm supposed to meet Sean around five. We're going sightseeing."

"At night? It'll be dark by then."

Yvonne shrugged. "That's what the brother said."

"You and Sean seem to be hitting it off real good," Adrianne said, with a raised brow. "What type of work does he do again?"

"Airplane, mechanical stuff. I forget."

"Um, not a lot of money in that." Adrianne yawned. "And what kind of ride is he rolling in?"

"Why?"

"Just wanted to know." Adrianne shut the door behind them.

"BMW," Yvonne replied.

"New or old?"

"Both," Yvonne said curtly. If he drove a hoopty, it shouldn't really make a difference, she was thinking. But then again, this was L.A.

"Um-hmm," Adrianne exasperated, opening the garage door. "We'll get you back in time, don't worry. Mikal wants us to stop by his house on our way home."

Yvonne closed her car door and locked it. "Mikal? For what?"

Adrianne started the engine, shifted the gear in reverse, and sped out of the garage. "Your guess is as good as mine." She gave a halfhearted wave to her next-door neighbor. "I suppose he wants to see you," she spouted, running through the stop sign posted at the front entrance. "And what Mikal wants, Mikal usually gets."

They pulled into the large circular cobblestone drive-way, encircled by a large black metal gate that had been left open. Several mature palm trees towered throughout the flawlessly manicured front lawn, giving the pastel colored minimansion an exotic appearance. A red, two-seater convertible Mercedes Benz, a mahogany Jaguar, and a charcoal gray and black Rolls-Royce sat parked on a forty-five-degree angle to the left of the house. Two colossal-sized dogs of undetermined breed raced toward the car, barking malevolently.

"Whose house is this?" Yvonne asked in wonderment. This view was better than sitting at a so-called posh restaurant with Fawn and Adrianne and their friend, Kala, rambling on and on about a man ain't worth nothing but the size of his wallet. Eyeing the dogs anxiously, she inhaled a choppy breath.

Adrianne parked the car in front of the house, near the twenty or so cement steps lined by a barrage of ivy plants. She opened the car door and stepped out of the car, patting the head of each dog as she did so.

"Are you coming?" she asked Yvonne.

Yvonne, stricken with fear of the dogs, cautiously stepped out of the car. One of the dogs, the male one to be specific, rushed over to her and began sniffing her private area. Timidly and unsuccessfully, she tried to shoo the dog away.

"Down, Kemo," a male voice ordered from behind. The dog backed away from Yvonne and sat down on the concrete. Mikal stepped outside of the door onto the landing.

"Sorry about that, Yvonne. He gets carried away sometimes," he was saying while walking down the steps.

"Yeah, like his owner," Adrianne replied under her breath.

"You ladies come on up." He was wearing a royal blue smoker's jacket and a matching pair of pants, stroking the neck of a tan and brown Siamese cat.

It was two forty-five in the afternoon. Why was he dressed like that? Yvonne thought, reaching the top of the landing. The smell of an expensive cologne that seemed to cheapen because of its heavy effect, bombarded her nose. Yvonne sneezed violently twice more than she normally did whenever something irritated her.

"Bless you," Mikal said, lowering the cat down onto the marble floor. "You allergic to cats?"

No, I'm allergic to too much Paco Raban, Yvonne wanted to say. But then she sneezed for the fifth time.

"Let me get you some Benadryl or something," Mikal said, climbing the spiral staircase before Yvonne had a chance to stop him. "Adrianne, you all go on into the den. You know where it is," he called out.

Yvonne followed Adrianne through a maze of corners and sharp angles, past the plush peach and brown living room with the suede and glass furniture, into the den where the black, baby grand piano sat.

"Wow. What does Mikal do?" Yvonne asked, wiping the wet corner of her eyes. She sat down on the other black leather chair-and-a-half, across from Adrianne, in awe at the exquisiteness of what she had seen so far. The room reminded her of zebra stripes, full of black and white furniture and pictures.

"He owns a business," Adrianne said, picking up the latest copy of *Robb's Report*.

"What kind of business?" Yvonne reached over and stroked the piece of sculpture sitting on the lacquered coffee table.

"Import, export—among some things," Adrianne replied, never lifting her eye from the magazine.

"Is he one of your clients?" Yvonne sneezed again.

"Yes," Adrianne replied flatly. "Bless you."

Yvonne sensed Adrianne's change in demeanor—had noticed it as soon as they rounded into the driveway, and when she neglected to answer the question about whose house it was they were pulling up to. Seemed like every time Adrianne got around Mikal, her disposition changed. Maybe there was something going on with them regarding business. She remembered Adrianne mentioning something about some tax questions when they were at Red Rooster on Wednesday night.

"What's wrong, Adrianne? You seem bothered."

Adrianne shut the magazine in frustration. If only Ms. Bright-Eyes had any idea. She was about to say as much when she saw Mikal walking into the room. "Nothing," is all she said.

"Here you go," Mikal said, handing Yvonne a glass of water and a white tablet wrapped in plastic casing, with Benadryl written across it. He had changed into a casual pair of slacks and a silk shirt.

"Thanks," Yvonne said, opening the packet. "I don't know what it is." She popped the pill in her mouth and swallowed it with the water. When she looked up again, she caught Mikal's intense piercing gaze.

"Probably allergies. L.A.'s air is full of bad stuff," Mikal said, sitting down on the piano bench. "How're you liking our city?"

"It's all right," Yvonne said, cutting her glare over toward Adrianne.

"She wigged out when she saw a low-rider bouncing down the main strip, sideways." Adrianne laughed.

Mikal chuckled. "What? They don't have any cars riding down the street on two wheels in your neck of the woods?"

"Not that I ever recall seeing." Yvonne smiled. "It did trip me out seeing a car gliding down a main avenue all twisted up like that."

"You'd be surprised how many folks got them old cars souped up like that. My bet?" Mikal said, with a raised brow. "It'll be a matter of time before you see it back East and the Southeast."

"That would be the day. I can only imagine seeing a sixty-eight Chevy low-riding, down the street, on two wheels in the snow." They all laughed.

"I made reservations at Panache for five thirty," Mikal

told them. "You all might want to go home—freshen up a bit."

Yvonne cut a puzzled look at Adrianne, who passed a confusing glance at Mikal. Did she miss something? What was Mikal talking about—he had reservations? After minutes of total quietness, except for the freshwater fish tank that was bubbling and gurgling in the background, Yvonne spoke up first.

"I already have plans this evening," she said, looking at Mikal.

"Cancel 'em." Mikal stood up and walked over toward Yvonne, relieving her of the empty glass of water she held. "It's not often you get tickets to the NAACP Image Awards. I figure we would eat dinner first."

Yvonne laughed inwardly. *Was he serious? Cancel my plans because he has tickets to the NAACP Image Awards? He's tee-ripping.* She repositioned herself in the chair, using her elbow and the arm of the chair to help straighten her posture.

"I wish I could, Mikal," she lied. "But I can't." Yvonne looked over at Adrianne, who looked like she had just seen a ghost.

Mikal stood tall and quiet, pondering Yvonne's words. "And it's more spectacular than attending the event of the year? Come, come, Yvonne," he spoke softly. "Surely whatever, or whomever, you have plans with would understand that this is a big deal, especially since you're new to L.A."

He chuckled uneasily. Such integrity. Under any other circumstances he'd find that disrespectful, almost pretentious even. But with Yvonne, he found it to be admirable, even if slightly annoying. Here she sat in the middle of his home, turning him down and shoving his offer back in his face. He would not give up so effortlessly.

"You can always go to dinner or to a movie or whatever it is you're going to do tomorrow. This is a big event," Mikal said, stretching his arms outward to exemplify his statement. "And I would like nothing more than you and Adrianne, of course, to attend the event with me. I'd be honored."

Yvonne blushed. How thoughtful of him, she surmised. Even if she didn't quite trust him. She glanced down at her square-faced watch with the faded, cowhide leather band. My, my, where does the time tick off to? It was three twenty-five. Sean would be at Adrianne's house in a little over an hour. She looked over at Adrianne, who was apparently preoccupied with her nailbed or something of that nature.

Smiling softly, illustrating a pure sense of gratitude, Yvonne said, "Thank you, Mikal, but I have to take a rain check. I really must keep this engagement." She touched his hand casually. "You can appreciate a lady keeping her word, can't you?"

"Only if she is sincere about allowing me to cash in my rain check." He smiled.

"We better get going if you want to be home by four," Adrianne said, rising from the sofa. "We've got a bit of a drive."

Yvonne rose from her chair as well, following Adrianne out of the room. "You have a nice home," she told Mikal when they reached the front door.

"Thank you," he said, opening the door. "I'll give you a tour the next time you come over."

"I'd like that. Thank you for the offer again. Have a great time." Yvonne descended the stairs, surprised to see that bodacious dog, Kemo, was still sitting in the same spot.

Adrianne was at the bottom of the steps, ready to get into the car, when Mikal beckoned her from the top of the landing.

"Oh, I forgot to give you that paperwork. I have it right in here," he said, walking back into the house.

"I'll be back," Adrianne said to Yvonne, who was already seated in the car.

Adrianne dashed up the stairs two at a time, despite the fact she was donned in tights and a miniskirt. She entered the hallway, expecting to see Mikal standing nearby. She walked farther into the house, searching for his presence. He had a way of jumping out of the smallest nook and scaring the crap out of her.

"Here you go," he whispered, startling her. He ripped out a check from his checkbook and handed it to her.

Hesitantly Adrianne grabbed the check and examined it. Three thousand dollars? She glanced up at Mikal, who was standing off in the corner in the dark, with a mirthless glower fixated upon his face. "I don't care how you do it, Adrianne. But you better make it happen. There's more for you when you do." He turned and headed up the stairs.

Adrianne wanted to holler, Why? What's the big deal? But her lips wouldn't obey—partly because she knew the answer to the question. It was just because he was Mikal Peralta. That's why. And as everyone in L.A. knows, beside Mikal being the richest and most powerful black man in the city, Mikal always gets what Mikal wants. She folded the check and tucked it inside her blouse, somewhere between her lace bra and the new breast that Mikal had paid for last year.

Stepping outside the front door, she caught a side profile

of Yvonne. The image was so innocent and pure it was almost fairy tale-like. She sighed a heavy breath. If only Yvonne had any idea what she had left back east to come to in the west, she would have stayed home. She opened her car door and sat down, wrestling the seat belt over her lap. Yvonne eyed her suspiciously. *Not to worry,* Yvonne, Adrianne thought turning the ignition. *What you don't know definitely won't hurt you.*

Eight

Sean parked the BMW and shifted the brake hand lever upward. The more and more time he spent with Yvonne, the more he could feel himself getting reeled in. The fluttering in the pit of his stomach increased as he strolled up the walkway of Adrianne's swank town house. Spending three evenings in a row with Yvonne, or any woman, was certainly out of character—as well as driving nearly an hour across town to reach her.

He wedged his index finger into the circular hole the size of a nickel. The doorbell chimed and he heard the patter of feet touching the corner patch of tile before the front door swung open. Adrianne posed in the arched doorway dressed in a navy and silver formal sequin gown. The split in the front of the thousand dollar, or more, dress exposed a healthy brown thigh arched in a pair of heels.

"Hello, Sean," She said a bit too seductively.

"Good evening," Sean sheepishly replied.

"Come on in," she said, partially blocking the doorway on purpose. "Yvonne is upstairs, trying to pull herself together." She stepped out of the way only after Sean brushed past her.

"Can I get you something to drink? Some juice? Wine? Champagne?"

"No thank you," he said, wandering down the short hall-way.

"Well," Adrianne sang. "I'm going to have a glass of something. You can have a seat in the living room if you like."

Sean entered the living room and took the first seat he could find. Hopefully Yvonne would come jogging down those stairs in the next few minutes. He didn't know how long he'd be able to stave off the all-so-flamboyant Adrianne, without totally crushing her little all-that ego.

Adrianne pranced into the living room, holding a goblet half-filled with champagne. She struck a pose next to the fireplace, next to all the dozens of pictures she had of the L.A. clique.

"I love the way an expensive champagne glides down my throat." She grinned coyly. How did Yvonne get to town and find such a handsome male friend already? Just like her, Adrianne fretted inwardly. Always got the men falling all over her. Not only Sean but now Mikal, too. Well, she wasn't going to have them both.

"What's the big occasion?" Sean asked, changing the direction of the conversation. Nothing personal, Adrianne, Sean said, to himself, but you ain't my type—got that L.A. thing going on.

"NAACP Image Awards," she said airily, taking another sip of champagne. "I'd thought a man of your stature would be there, too." Her eyes rested down at his crotch. Damn—he's one fine caramel-coated brother. Bet he's good in bed, too. She lifted her eyes away from the lower portion of his pants and moved them down to his spit-shined shoes. Um, she sighed inwardly. She could wrap her legs around that broad back of his anytime, anywhere.

A man of my stature? Cute, Sean thought. "I'll catch it

on TV in a couple of weeks. Commercials and all." He smiled tightly. If Yvonne didn't hurry up and get her fine behind down them stairs, Adrianne would surely be lunging at him.

The room grew stuffy, like a vacationer returning home to a clamped-up house. If he was a betting man, he would have never figured Yvonne and Adrianne to be cut from the slightest piece of the same cloth. There Adrianne stood with too much makeup and way too much weave.

"Oh," Adrianne said, placing her glass atop of the mantelpiece. "Can you be a dear, Sean, and fasten this little hook for me?" she asked, turning her back to face him. "My nails are too long, and Yvonne . . ." She paused. "Well, she ain't the best-coordinated person."

Sean remained seated. This request was certainly off-limits, he thought, sending off a quick prayer that Yvonne would come toppling down those stairs right now. What in the world was taking her so long anyway? They were only going to cruise some of Los Angeles' tourist places, get a bite to eat, and maybe grab a movie. Was she dressing for the NAACP Image Awards, too?

Realizing that Sean was not going to partake in her invitation to step into her personal space, smell the sweetness or her scent, and maybe even feel the softness of her skin, she turned to face him.

"I won't bite you, Sean," she said coyly. "I just need to have this hook fastened so that the top of my dress doesn't fall down and show off these thirty-four D's."

Sean rubbed both his hands across the thighs of his pants. He could see the hook from where he sat, and from the looks of it, her top might drop down if she didn't get that clasp fastened. Doubtfully he rose from the love seat, making his way over toward her, glancing at the stairs the entire time. He stood behind Adrianne, whose head was bent forward, exposing the nape of her neck. Quickly he grasped the clasp, trying hard to complete the request before Yvonne bounced down the stairs. But the darn little metal fastener wouldn't cooperate.

"Can you feel it?" Adrianne asked.

"Yes," Sean replied. "If I can just . . ." The clasp slipped through his fingers again. He attempted a third time, which proved to be the definite charm. "Got it," he said, stepping backward—out of her immediate personal space.

"Oh, thank you, Sean," Adrianne exasperated loudly, slinging her arms around his neck. "Thank you so much." She planted an unexpected kiss on his lips just before looking over his shoulder at a stunned Yvonne, standing at the bottom of the steps. "Oh," she said smoothly. "Hi, Yvonne."

Sean swirled around to face Yvonne, the ruby-colored lipstick still tinting his lips. "Hey," he said awkwardly. "I was just helping Adrianne get her outfit together."

Yvonne smiled tensely. "Hey," she said gruffly. She didn't want to make a big scene about what she thought she saw. Certainly there was a good explanation for what happened other than all men being dogs and barking and sniffing up the skirt of any woman who would be willing. Surely there was nothing to Adrianne placing a bold kiss on Sean's lips right in front of her.

"You ready?" Sean asked, feeling a little uncomfortable. He stood scanning Yvonne's body language, hoping that she would not mistake what took place as an act of malice on his part. A few seconds elapsed before the ringing of the telephone soaked the atmosphere.

"Sure," Yvonne said, slinging her pocketbook across her shoulder.

"You two have a good time," Adrianne said.

The first few minutes of the drive were quieter than the never-ending stroll down the walkway toward the car. After three or four annoying commercial jingles about oil changes, fried chicken, and soda, Sean pushed in a CD. Kirk Whalum's saxophone filtered through the expensive speakers.

A wild saxophone note stirred throughout the car. The silence between him and Yvonne was killing him. He wanted to explain, go into more detail about what had taken place back at Adrianne's house but decided it would be a moot point. Besides that, he hadn't done anything wrong. Had he?

"Your cousin, Adrianne, is overwhelming—very forward," Sean finally said.

Yvonne nodded her head. She said nothing, just gently swayed to the jingle. She read the blue and red print of a billboard, advertising some new sports beverage, as they continued to drive silently.

Okay. Enough is enough, Sean decided. If he had to be the one to break the silence between them, then damn it, he was going to break it. The chicken jingle that had filled the car a few minutes earlier replayed in his head. "How come our brothers and sisters are always singing about chicken and hamburgers?" He laughed artificially. "Are we the only culture who sings about everything we purchase? Like spending money is our major goal in life."

Yvonne raised a thought-provoking brow. Maybe she was making way too much of what she saw. Knowing Adrianne, she had intentionally kissed Sean in an attempt to get her goat, like she had done so many times during their upbringing. Probably a warped sense of payback for Mikal having paid too much attention to her earlier.

Still needing a verbal response from Yvonne, Sean continued. "I mean, spouting off some soulful song about an oil change . . ." He paused to mimic the commercial that had just gone off. "Are we still only good enough for our singing?"

"Yes," Yvonne said lowly. "And our dancing." She rocked her head back and forth to another of Kirk's songs. It had been too many weeks since she had a chance to teach her dance class to a group of kids. Dancing had become her only mode of solace—of escaping and dancing away any and all of her troubles. She sure hoped that Adrianne would keep her promise and take her to church Sunday so they could meet the minister in charge of dance.

Sean watched her wiggle in her seat from the corner of his eyes. "You want to dance, don't you?"

Yvonne nodded enthusiastically, still bobbing her head to the music. "Can't help it. It's in my bones."

"Then we'll have to find a way to rattle them bones of yours tonight. And I know just exactly how to do it." Sean grinned slyly. The perplexed look on Yvonne's face told him that she was uncertain about his comment. Well, not to worry, Yvonne, Sean thought. You're in good hands with me.

Sean and Yvonne walked hand in hand to the end of the boardwalk, bundled tightly together, sharing in each other's warmth, while warding off the brisk wind. The gushing sounds of the waves cresting and crashing against the pillars beneath them, and the electric blue hue of the moon bouncing off the water, set for a quixotic scene.

Yvonne barely shivered. Pressing the side of her body into Sean, dampness penetrated through the ribbed, cotton sweater she wore beneath Sean's leather bomber jacket.

And even with all that additional padding, she could still feel the salt air tickling the hairs on the back of her neck.

Too much sweating at the dance club was responsible for the moisture flanking his body. Sean stood bravely, with just a sleeveless undershirt beneath a long-sleeved, cotton and rayon shirt tucked into a pair of jeans, trembling internally. Chivalry was not something he could ever erase. It was part of his makeup, his childhood, his father.

"Did you enjoy yourself at the club?" he asked Yvonne, tucking his free hand into his pants pocket.

"Absolutely," she uttered softly. "Dancing is therapeutic for me." She attempted to speak some more but clamped her teeth together instead, making a shivering sound.

"Let's go back to the car. We can do this some other time, when it isn't forty-nine degrees outside," Sean said, turning around to head back toward the car.

"Exactly," Yvonne agreed happily. "And when I don't have to freeze you in the meantime by wearing your clothes." She slid the jacket off her shoulder and handed it back to Sean.

"Naw, naw," Sean said, with an exaggerated shivering sound in his voice. "You keep it until we get to the car. No sense in us both freezing to death," he stammered with a partial chuckle. "What we need is some hot chocolate, indoor heat, and a piece of pecan pie."

"Pecan pie?" Yvonne repeated. "I thought you were a sweet-potato pie man?"

"At this point, I'm any-ol-kinda-pie man," Sean said with a grin and pulling the car keys out of his pocket. The dollar green Beemer was parked only a few feet away from them.

Yvonne smiled, taking his offered hand to help her step

down the four or five logs that served as a stepping stone toward the end of the boardwalk pier. Easily she came tumbling down into the softness of the heavy, lumpy sand. Lordy, Lordy, she was beginning to fall in heavy-like with Sean. He was a great cure for her mending heart. She hadn't thought about Desmond or Danni for several days. If she wasn't careful, she could find herself totally captivated by Sean Germaine.

Sean moved ahead of Yvonne, when they reached the car, so that he could unlock her side of the car door. He stuck the key in the lock. Stopping suddenly, he turned and grabbed her by the waist and drew her into his chest, before pressing his lips atop hers. The heat of her breath and tongue rushed to his head immediately, causing him to lean against the car for support, as he reeled her closer into his bosom.

Their tongues danced together. Yvonne could feel the passion rising inside her. And she could most certainly feel Sean's response to such passion rising and pressing against her inner thigh. Lordy, Lordy, she thought. If she was in a different mind, she could make love to this man right here and right now. Taking a moment of reprieve, Yvonne wiped the plum-colored stain from Sean's succulent lips. She and Sean? This level of desire so soon? The ability to mesh so nicely together on such a quick and unsuspecting note? This was way too crazy—like one of those pocket-sized romance books. She sighed.

They stood embraced in each other's arms for many minutes more. Surprisingly the wetness that had penetrated through them earlier, as the salt water chill lingered in the air, ceased to exist. The sounds of the ocean roaring in the black of night rang its own song—a song that Yvonne and Sean swayed to together.

"What's on your agenda for tomorrow?" Sean asked, kissing her forehead.

"Adrianne and I are supposed to go to church in the morning and then I guess brunch afterward. But that's it. My day is fairly open after that. Although I do need to spend some time getting prepared for my meeting with the firm on Monday. Why? What's on your agenda?"

"I've got a meeting for my job in the morning. Then I'll head out of town for a week for some additional training in the late afternoon."

"Didn't you just get back from being out of town?"

"That was personal. This is business," he said, kissing her forehead again. "Not to worry. I'll be calling you a couple of times during the week, if not every day while I'm gone."

"I'm not worried," Yvonne told him. "Just didn't want to get too addicted to these kisses if you know you'll be on the road often."

"I heard that," Sean said, kissing her again. He could tell by that Kodaklike gloss filtering over her eyes that she was feeling it like he was. His disposition soured suddenly. Did he really want this? Want to be responsible for someone else's feelings about him again? Didn't he vow not to let that ever happen again? Wasn't that tragic experience traumatic enough for him?

No, he would not let Yvonne love him so deeply, like he had let Natalie all those years ago. Though he liked Yvonne more than he cared to admit, he had to restrain himself from letting the feelings get any deeper. The timing of this trip was perfect. It would give him a chance to get a grip on this Yvonne thing.

He studied her face more intensely. She seemed like a pretty reasonable and stable woman. Even in the midst of her hurtful situation with her engagement breakup, she appeared to have maintained her cool. He brushed a gentle hand across her cheek, Yes, Yvonne did seem to be a rational person. But so did Natalie.

Sean sighed unintentionally. "You feel like a little hot chocolate and some dessert?" He had slipped his hands down the side of her hips, before removing them altogether. He turned away suddenly, opening the car door.

"Sounds good," she said, getting into the car. "I've danced off enough calories tonight to afford a late-night snack."

Sean shut the door behind her, walked over to his side of the car, and got in. He flipped over the ignition and started the car, quickly sliding the temperature lever from the cool side to the hot. Regina Belle's sultry voice crooned through the car. Sean shuddered. He snuck a quick peek at Yvonne as she stared out the window, singing the lyrics to the song.

He was vacillating. No doubt about it. *Yvonne is such a beautiful sister.* He shifted the car into reverse. *And so levelheaded. Certainly she didn't illustrate any behavioral problems. But then neither did Natalie . . . in the beginning.* He shook his head in attempt to clear his thoughts, before placing the car into drive and accelerating forward. He flipped on the blinker, turned onto the desolate street thinking, *but then again, Sean, suicide ain't something that's predictable.*

Nine

Adrianne wheeled her car between a 1972 Oldsmobile Cutlass and a fairly new Acura Legend, stopping so suddenly in the tight parking space that her and Yvonne's heads snapped backward. She glanced into the rearview mirror, realigned her sunglasses, tousled her hair a few more times, then stepped out of the car.

Yvonne followed suit, only she didn't take time out to guarantee that her frock was as posh as Adrianne's. Much of that had to do with her easy hairstyle. Thank God for Bantu knots. She watched as Adrianne sorted through her pocketbook for something or another before searching the backseat of the car. Yvonne stood at the back of the car, patiently waiting for her cousin to complete her fickle procedure—a definite trademark.

Adrianne had always been a wannabe star and limelight pursuer since they were young adults. She was the person crowned with most popular in high school and the person most likely to succeed. She had joined the drama club, the fashion club, the drill team, and the cheerleading squad. All in the hopes of being discovered.

"Have you seen my leather-bound Bible?" Adrianne mumbled. She flipped the front seat forward to get a better view of the space beneath it.

"You had it in your hand when you came downstairs this morning," Yvonne replied, walking over toward her.

Adrianne shuffled some more items under her seat, including a black leather pouch with the metal snap. She shoved it under the seat quickly.

"What's that?" Yvonne asked.

"My piece," Adrianne sat matter-of-factly.

"Your piece? As in a gun?"

"Yeah," Adrianne replied, still searching for her Bible.

"What do you need with a gun?"

"Everybody is strapped in L.A. Don't trip. It's registered."

"Is it loaded?"

"Maybe," Adrianne answered sarcastically.

"You leave it in the car?"

"No, I meant to bring it into the house. I leave it in my nightstand. But I was meeting a client in Englewood day before yesterday, and I guess I forgot to take it in." She stood erect again. "Well, I don't see it. Let me think." She sighed. "Maybe I set it on the table by the front door when I went out to grab the newspaper. No matter—you have your Bible, right?"

"Right," Yvonne said, holding up her hardbound NIV Bible. Funny the way it seemed quite normal to discuss a gun and a Bible all in the same sentence, Yvonne thought, lagging behind Adrianne.

Glistening sunrays beat down on the faded, stubble pavement as Yvonne and Adrianne began to make their long journey to one of the most popular churches in the Los Angeles area. Sunday morning on Crenshaw Boulevard was a ritual in itself. Various cars cruised the notorious avenue, pumping an array of sounds from Kirk Franklin & the Family to Tupac. Smells of fried chicken and hash browns and buttermilk pancakes and The Chronic wafted throughout the air.

Yvonne purposely dragged her left foot across the pavement in a failed attempt to free the sole of her leather sling-backs from the pink wad of bubble gum. She hissed in frustration before using the curbside, where she and Adrianne stood waiting for the light, to help remove the gum.

"Why didn't we park in the Crenshaw Central Baptist church parking lot?" Yvonne asked, looking up at a plump, elderly man sitting behind the wheel of a new Cadillac. "There was plenty of parking back there."

"Because those spaces are reserved for the stars. Like Magic & Cookie, Gladys Knight, and Les Brown, and Debbie Allen and Norm. People like that," Adrianne said, hurrying across the street with elongated strides.

"That's ridiculous and very unfair," Yvonne said, also quickening her pace. "Who determines that their soul is more important than mine?"

"What are you talking about now?" Adrianne asked with a puzzled look on her face.

"I'm talking about this." Yvonne illustrated with her hands at nothing in particular. "Us walking nearly a mile to get to the church because the available parking spaces in the church lot are off-limits for normal folks like you and me."

"Speak for yourself," Adrianne said tartly. "The church should accommodate the stars. Can you imagine them trying to walk all this way to the church without being stopped by every Tom, Dick, and Harry?" She chortled. "Get over it, Yvonne. You could probably use the exercise anyway. And a little dose of reality," Adrianne murmured under her breath.

"What's that comment supposed to mean?"

"Means nothing," Adrianne told her, reaching another street to cross. "Nothing at all."

"It must mean something for you to say that to me." Yvonne pushed some more.

"It's just that you've still got that naive way about you. That's all," Adrianne told her. "This is L.A.—the real world, Yvonne. Money is the motivating factor—lots of people here have lots of it. And more importantly, money buys power and prestige. And parking spaces."

Adrianne stepped into the crosswalk, sashaying purposely, causing the driver of an oncoming car to slam on his brakes. The skidding sound startled her. She continued with her gait amid the blare of the horn and the rumbling of curse words.

Having finally crossed the intersection in pure climactic style, she headed toward the Burger King parking lot where a bevy of brothers huddled around, absorbing a slice of life on Crenshaw Boulevard. The heckling and catcalls had already begun earlier that morning, as the crowd of young boys taunted a few of the church members walking past the fast-food restaurant in order to get to the ten thousand-member church.

Yvonne was walking stride for stride with Adrianne by the time they reached the church. Yvonne's eyes widened when she noted the lengthy line of folks wrapped around the corner. All these people going to the same church? Suddenly the long-anticipated need of attending church and speaking with the pastor about offering dance classes to kids in the neighborhood didn't seem so majestic.

Yvonne glanced down at her watch. 10:20 A.M. "Are all these people waiting to get into the eleven o'clock service?"

"Yup," Adrianne said, approaching the line. "Don't worry, we're not going to be standing in this line."

"We're not?" Yvonne felt a twinge of relief whiz through her. She had never had to wait in a line like this when she attended her church service in Atlanta.

"No," Adrianne said, flashing her radiant smile as she brushed past the line of folks diligently standing in line. "Just follow me."

After a few knocks and bumps and a few "pardon mes" and "excuse us," Adrianne and Yvonne reached the front entrance of the church. Two of the deacons stood staunchly, blocking off the entrance.

"Can I help you, sisters?" the tallest deacon, evidently in charge of security, asked them.

"Yes. We need to use the rest room," Adrianne said, with a counterfeit twinge of sincerity.

"Both of you?"

"Yes," Adrianne said tersely. "Please, before I embarrass myself," she said with flailed hands.

Brother deacon gave them a doubtful once-over—Adrianne in her improper, short, rust-colored dress and Yvonne in her prim and proper, navy blue, touching-the-knee dress, before stepping to the side and allowing them to pass through.

Adrianne could feel his eyes following their steps toward the rest room, so she didn't deviate from the contrived plan at first. Slyly looking back over her shoulder, and realizing that the deacon had gone on with the business of outside, she grabbed Yvonne by the arm and quickly scooped her across the hall to the prayer room.

"Just bow down and pray," she whispered, shutting the door behind her. "We'll be able to get a seat in the main part of the church if we stay here until service starts."

Adrianne fled Yvonne's side toward an empty plush, mauve, unoccupied Queen Anne chair, where she knelt down to pray.

Yvonne walked past three elderly sisters with colorful and view-restricting hats, toward an extended bench with the same matching material as the Queen Anne chair. The room was hot and stingy with its three chairs and two benches and three small tables, cramped in less than four hundred square feet. The elderly sisters, probably mothers of the church, were already humming their praise and worship tunes, edifying Jesus in that traditional *halle-luuuujah* way.

Fifteen minutes and forty "praise hims" later, Adrianne tapped Yvonne, who was deeply involved in a heavy inner dialogue with God, on the shoulder.

Dear Heavenly Father, Yvonne was praying silently. *Thank you for all that you have done in my life. Thank you for bringing me out of the fire—thank you for my slow healing regarding my breakup with Desmond. Thank you for seeing eyes to see and hearing ears to hear. Thank you for blessing me with the gift to dance. I even thank you for letting me get through law school—even though I can't seem to pass the bar.* Yvonne smiled at her last comment. A few tears drizzled her cheeks.

She hadn't looked up right away when Adrianne touched her—instead choosing to complete her requests and amens before rising from bent knees. She swiped her eyes with the knuckle of her index finger before reaching for the box of tissue propped on one of the nearby tables.

Lordy, Lordy, she felt like a world of weight had been lifted off her soul when she followed Adrianne out into the hallway, which was already crowded with church members. Her message from God seemed clear enough and fairly reachable, considering she was some three thousand miles across the country. Yes, she would try very hard to discard the hatred she had built up for Desmond and Danni over the past few weeks. She had to. Furthermore, harboring such malevolence would clearly restrict her from enjoying her newfound, reveling friendship with Sean.

The red velvet roped area marked "reserved" unnerved Yvonne as she and Adrianne maneuvered their way toward the seats in the middle section of the sanctuary. Why couldn't they sit up front—in the first five rows roped off? This was ridiculous, Yvonne thought, taking her seat next to Adrianne.

"Let me guess," Yvonne whispered under her breath. "Those seats up front are for the stars, right?"

Adrianne nodded her head yes. "And for the members of the church who pay much tithes and offering."

"Well, how come you're not up there?" Yvonne smiled.

"Because I don't tithe with money. I tithe with my time. I volunteer by keeping the church books," Adrianne happily added.

"One thing has nothing to with the other, Adrianne. You're still supposed to give ten percent of your gross income."

"Yeah?" Adrianne said, with raised brows, as the deacon stood at the pulpit and greeted the church members. "And the Bible also makes reference to being a joyful giver when you tithe." She smirked. "I don't tithe 'cause I would not be joyful." With that, Adrianne and Yvonne stood with the rest of the congregation to join in with the praise and worship songs.

Adrianne was too preoccupied with observing the Hollywood stars, strolling down the aisle toward the front of the church, to be committed to the worship of God. What seemed more important, more pressing, was the reason why one of the "Fresh Prince of Bel-Air" stars was wearing that drab, boring dress. And why was Mikal, an obvious top church tithe giver, trying to work his way into the empty seat next to Yvonne when he normally sat up front in the corded-off areas?

Adrianne exhaled a stifled breath when a tall, lanky sister with a practically shaven head beat Mikal to the seat. What was he trying to do anyway? How many times had she tried to tell Mikal that her cousin Yvonne was not interested and off-limits? But how could she say no to Mikal Peralta? Nobody said no to Mikal Peralta. Not her, not the pastor of Crenshaw Central Baptist, and not half the women in Los Angeles.

"How did you enjoy the sermon?" Adrianne asked Yvonne, pulling her along by the elbow in a hurried manner.

"It was okay. A lot more singing than sermon. Something I have to get used to."

"Well, we'll try a different church next Sunday."

Yvonne withdrew her elbow from Adrianne's grasp once they reached the hallway. "I would like to come back here next week. Seems like the spirit was moving here despite all the glitz and glamour." Yvonne chuckled.

"I guess. Listen," Adrianne said, eyeing through the crowd. "Let's get out of here and grab something to eat. I'm starving."

"I was hoping I could speak to the minister of youth programs about offering some dance classes here if I decide to stay in Los Angeles."

Adrianne pulled out her sunglasses and shoved them on

her face before walking outside. "Well, once you decide, I can set up an appointment with the pastor's secretary and we can go from there. But right now, I want to go from here and get somewhere that is serving a hefty brunch." She walked briskly ahead.

Yvonne quickened her steps, catching up to Adrianne. "What's wrong with you, Adrianne?"

"Nothing," Adrianne replied. "Just come on."

Halfway down the block, they heard the series of short honks from a horn. A horn that definitely did not belong to an American-made car. Actually the horn sounded familiar—sounded like a Jaguar—sounded like Mikal, Adrianne determined. Intent on ignoring the beep, thinking and hoping that it was some young brothers out to grab their attention, Adrianne reached the corner and veered right with Yvonne trailing slightly behind.

The male voice bellowing from the car finally caught Adrianne's attention. She turned to face the car with the well-known driver and his recognizable voice. Just as she thought, it was Mikal Peralta. Her face drooped when he pulled to the curb ahead of them and stepped out of the car.

"Ya'll didn't hear me blowing?" Mikal asked.

"We thought you'd be some weirdo," Adrianne said flatly. "We had no idea it was you," she lied, looking him in the eye. He was dressed to kill like always—in an Italian designer suit with matching shirt, tie, shoes, and socks. God, he was a handsome man, a man that she wouldn't mind having as her man—solely.

"How you doing this beautiful Sunday afternoon, Yvonne?" Mikal asked.

"Just fine, Mikal."

"Nothing less than the best. Philippians 4:8-9. Did you

enjoy this morning's service, Yvonne?" Mikal locked eyes with Yvonne again.

"It was compelling."

"Compelling?" He laughed. "Definitely an East Coast-slash-Atlanta flavor to that. I was about to grab some brunch. Why don't ya'll join me?"

Adrianne's stomach dropped. "I think Yvonne has plans already," she told Mikal. "Aren't you and Sean supposed to have lunch?" she asked, facing Yvonne.

Yvonne hesitated. "No. He's out of town. Remember?"

"Oh, that's right," Adrianne said stiffly. "Actually, Mikal, we were on our way to Fawn's house for brunch." She lied again.

"We'll invite her, too. Come on, Yvonne," he said, waving toward Adrianne, too. "I'll give you a ride to your car. You can follow me to the Hilton. They have a good brunch over there."

Reluctantly Yvonne got into the front seat of the spacious Jaguar, with its customized leather upholstery and spiffy gold rims. The crystal clear sounds of Take Six's acappella song was playing in the background. A sweet, floral scent coming from the dangling air-freshener swept past her nostrils. This was the most plush car she had been in since she had gone to dinner with Aunt Gigi and one of her male friends in his late-model Mercedes Benz. Even Sean's three series BMW didn't quite measure up to this.

"I'm in the lot behind the dry cleaners," Adrianne told him.

Mikal pulled into the gravel lot still impeded with dozens of cars parked in any which way possible. "Yvonne, you can ride with me if you like."

Yvonne looked at Mikal, then back at Adrianne, who was standing outside of the car, waiting for her. No, she would feel much more comfortable riding with Adrianne. She opened the car door and proceeded to step out.

Mikal reached over and softly placed his hand atop her arm. "I would really like it if you kept me company, Yvonne."

Yvonne looked down at her arm in surprise at the way he took comfort in touching her. There was something weird about the way his touch made her feel. His familiarity with her was slightly uneasy even though it made her feel special—important. She glanced into his handsome face. He was definitely one of those mesmerizing pretty boy types—the types she normally steered clear of, if she could help it.

Yvonne flashed a warm smile at Mikal, then said, "Nothing personal, Mikal, but I'm going to ride with Adrianne." She didn't completely trust her mixed emotions about Mikal. Something about his personality was adventurous, or slightly dangerous. And until she could get a handle on where he was coming from, she thought it best to steer clear of being alone with him. At least for now. She broadened her smile. "We'll see you at the restaurant," she said, gently shutting the car door behind her.

Mikal sat in the car eyeing Yvonne and that grandma dress she was wearing, as she walked with Adrianne to the car. Damn it, he thought slamming the steering wheel. Yvonne had about one more chance to reject him. Just one more. After that, he would use whatever means necessary to shake some sense into her—to help her recognize that she had no say in the matter. She was going to be the newest member of his flock.

Ten

Yvonne closed her left eye as she stroked the lid with Mary Kay's ginger spice eye shadow a second time before applying a new coat of cinnamon lipstick. The smell of burnt popcorn from the night before still lingered about the house like flies at a barbecue. Working a microwave had never been a problem before—never challenged her intelligence, until last night.

While waiting and hoping for Sean to call, she had placed a bag of lightly buttered popcorn in the microwave on high for five minutes. How was she to know that the high on Adrianne's microwave was really extra high? Needless to say that the blackened kernels and no phone call from Sean for the fourth night in a row were sure signs that things were not going as well as she had liked.

Pressing the blush brush into the smooth powder, Yvonne rubbed above each cheekbone area with the earthtone color. If it was that time of the year where a mild tan from the sun was do-able, she would easily be the first person lying out, with a good fiction book, on Adrianne's spacious patio. But it wasn't the roller-blading-down-Venice-Beach-with-just-a-bikini-on time of the year yet in Los Angeles.

The sun had chosen to find refuge behind the rolling clouds looming about the city at 9:35 A.M. in the morning.

Yvonne hustled from the hall bathroom into the guest bedroom with just her bra and a pair of matching panties hidden by the half-slip with the splits up each side. Maneuvering around L.A. on mass transit wasn't her favorite thing to do in this city by any means. But until she determined beyond a reasonable doubt that Los Angeles was to be her new home, there was no sense in shipping her car way across country.

First thing on the agenda was finding gainful employment in the legal industry. The interview with Douglass's friend and fraternity brother, Glenn, had gone surprisingly smooth. Except for his sly innuendoes thrown in every so often about if she got too lonely in such a big city, he'd be happy to help her out, Yvonne felt pretty darn good about the law clerk position.

This morning was the second and hopefully final interview of the hiring process. Today she had to meet with the firm's most prominent partner, Lucille Carter-White, a sister, who she heard could chew metal nails, swallow them, and comfortably digest them without so much as blinking.

She couldn't afford to be late for this interview—that's why she had gotten up right as Adrianne was leaving at 8:28 A.M. this morning to get prepared for the meeting. Grabbing her pantyhose, she sat on the chair facing the window. What a drab, cloudy morning, she thought, stretching out the packaged pair of putty-colored pantyhose.

She watched the leaves of the tall palm tree wave back and forth violently. A squirrel, intent on not being swept off the thin branch of a redwood tree by the gusting winds, clawed on for dear life. A neighbor's plastic garbage can top scraped across the concrete driveway, while another neighbor in the complex raced after a piece of paper sailing through the air.

Yvonne leaned back against the plush chair, contemplating the past two weeks of her new life as an L.A. resident. Except for meeting Sean, whom she hadn't heard from in almost a week, she didn't see what all the hype was about L.A. He said he was going out of town for a week and that he would call, and she believed him. But now that the days were turning into nights and still no call from Sean, she was beginning to second guess their rendezvous.

Perhaps he would call later on tonight. That would be a good thing, Yvonne thought, placing her left foot into the pantyhose. Hearing the telephone ringing a second time, she hurried over toward the night table where the phone lay. She had to answer by the end of the third ring or else Adrianne's answering machine would catch it. And she would have to wait for Adrianne to get home to get the message if it were for her because the machine was in Adrianne's room. Adrianne was so particular about her room, and her stuff, that Yvonne refused to enter it to borrow a Band-Aid if she needed without Adrianne's consent.

Yvonne fell against the bed, after hustling across to the other side of the room to answer the telephone. She lifted the phone receiver and spouted, "Good morning."

"Morning, honey," Aunt Gigi said in her bubbly voice. "Hope I didn't catch you sleeping in."

"Not at all, Aunt Gigi," Yvonne said happily. "I'm getting ready for my second interview with White, Trimble, and Tate. Got to meet with the queen bee today."

"Oooh, the queen bee, huh? Well, I'll bc sure to say a prayer for you. How's everything else? Am I going to have to put your name and L.A. address and phone number in ink?"

"Not yet, Auntie. I'm still in the checking-out stages. How are things with you?"

"Fine, fine. You know me, honey, ain't much going to stop your aunt Gigi." She laughed some. "How are you and your new friend doing?"

"Sean?"

"Why, is there someone else?"

"No, not really. Actually," Yvonne said, trying to place the other part of the pantyhose on her right leg. "I haven't heard from him in a few days."

"Really?"

"Yeah. He mentioned something about going out of town for his job for a week. But he sounded so sure that he would call me the minute he got to his destination. I hope nothing is wrong."

"Sweetheart, him being a man in the first place is wrong in itself." Aunt Gigi laughed. "Give it another day or two. He may still call. If not, later for him. Besides, you've got more important things to deal with other than a man. How soon is the firm looking to hire you?"

"I haven't gotten the job yet, Aunt Gigi," Adrianne said, taking a break from struggling with the pantyhose.

"Oh, but you will. Anyway," Aunt Gigi said, between a yawn. "I probably shouldn't be telling you this, but I think you deserve to know. I bumped into Desmond yesterday evening."

There was a lengthy pause—a moment where nothing but the sounds of that garbage can lid screeching across the pavement filled the other portion of her mind. *Bumped into Desmond yesterday?* Yvonne replayed in the free part of her mind again.

"He gave me a message to give to you," Aunt Gigi enlightened.

Yvonne still didn't say a word. A surge of emotions zipped through her body, ranging from sadness to nothing to anger. How dare him give a message through you, Aunt Gigi. Forget him and that heifer Danni Green.

"What?" Yvonne finally said.

"He told me to tell you that he is sorry. That he really didn't mean for things to happen the way they did. That he still loves you very much, and that he and Danni, despite her claim, will never be together. And that he's going to take a paternity test to be sure."

"Well, ain't that grand? He wouldn't have had to take a paternity test if he'd kept his johnson in his pants," Yvonne responded crassly.

"I'm sorry, sugar. I probably should have just kept my big mouth closed. I hope you're not terribly upset with me."

"Not at all, Aunt Gigi. I'm just angry with Desmond and his weak apology. Did he mention my money?"

"He owes you some money? How much?"

Yvonne shut her eyes. She didn't want to bring Aunt Gigi into this. She was struggling with her own financial upheaval.

"Never mind, Aunt Gigi," Yvonne said, opening her eyes. "I'll handle it."

She glanced at the clock radio. 10:00 A.M. Oh Lord, her appointment was scheduled for eleven fifteen. Had she been talking to Aunt Gigi that long? Lordy, Lordy, how was she going to get way across town on a public bus in time for her interview?

The other phone line clicked, signaling another call was coming in. It was time to end the conversation anyway.

Get 4 **FREE** Arabesque Contemporary Romances Delivered to Your Doorstep and Join the Only New Book Club That Delivers These Bestselling African American Romances Directly to You Each Month!

No Obligation!

WE INVITE YOU TO JOIN THE ONLY BOOK
CLUB THAT DELIVERS HEARTFELT ROMANCE
FEATURING AFRICAN AMERICAN HEROES AND
HEROINES IN STORIES THAT ARE RICH IN
PASSION AND CULTURAL SPICE...

And Your First 4 Books Are FREE!

Arabesque is the newest contemporary romance line offered by
Pinnacle Books. Arabesque has been so successful that our
readers have asked us about direct home delivery. We
responded to your requests. You can start receiving four
bestselling Arabesque novels a month delivered right to your
door. Subscribe now and you'll get:

- 4 FREE Arabesque romances as our introductory gift—a value
  of almost $20! (pay only $1 to help cover postage &
  handling)
- 4 BRAND-NEW Arabesque romances
  delivered to your doorstep each month
  thereafter (usually arriving before
  they're available in bookstores!)
- 20% off each title—a savings of
  almost $4.00 each month
- FREE home delivery
- A FREE monthly newsletter,
  Zebra/Pinnacle Romance News that
  features author profiles, book previews
  and more
- No risks or obligations...in other words, you can cancel
  whenever you wish with no questions asked

So subscribe to Arabesque today and see why these books are
winning awards and readers' hearts.

After you've enjoyed our FREE gift of 4 Arabesques, you'll begin
to receive monthly shipments of the newest Arabesque titles.
Each shipment will be yours to examine for 10 days. If you
decide to keep the books, you'll pay the preferred subscriber's
price of just $4.00 per title. That's $16 for all 4 books with
FREE home delivery! And if you want us to stop sending books,
just say the word...it's that simple.

*See why reviewers are raving about ARABESQUE
and order your FREE books today!*